# THE DELTIC DISASTER

## AND OTHER TALES

Jeff Vawter

Published by New Generation Publishing in 2019



First Edition



**www.newgeneration-publishing.com**

Dedicated to the hard-working railway preservationists
in Great Britain

*"...Or as a traveller, who has gained the brow*
*Of some aerial Down, while there he halts*
*For breathing-time, is tempted to review*
*The region left behind him; and if aught*
*Deserving notice have escaped regard,*
*Or been regarded with too careless eye,*
*Strives, from that height, with one and yet one more*
*Last look, to make the best amends he may:*
*So have we lingered."*

The Prelude, Book Ninth,
William Wordsworth

## CONTENTS

## CHAPTER ONE
# The Deltic Disaster

A scheme to help commemorate the fine (?) service of the Deltic engines ended up quite differently than expected.

A rail tour was planned and organized by the six members of DOSE (Deltic Observers and Steady Enthusiasts), along with the assistance of a professional, to run from Paddington to Broadlands Halt and return. The trip was scheduled to leave on a Saturday morning in May and return that afternoon. The engine that was to be used was one of the first built, dubbed 'Old Rust and Rivets' by its unenthusiastic crews. Of course, no one in DOSE ever heard the engine referred to in this manner. To do so would have meant a sure sack and a good wigging.

To further increase sales and ensure a full consist, the promoter and organizer, Ian McSwindle, hit upon a dubious plan which advertised that, in addition to the excursion itself, an expedition would be undertaken to find the elusive Danny-in-the-Dales. According to legend, Danny-in-the-Dales is an elfish-like creature, clad in green (but no relation to the infamous outlaw further north), has reddish hair, and sparkling blue eyes. Several times a year, in spring and fall, Danny appears on top of a hillside during a night blessed with a full moon. He skips and dances his way across the rolling hills, then suddenly turns into the dales below. It is believed that if one follows Danny to his secret abode, one will discover a score (or more) of large black pots filled with gold sovereigns.

This quaint and amusing legend helped to draw 120 applicants for tickets. However, exactly 101 people, including DOSE, showed up to purchase them for 150 pounds each. Lodging was said to be provided at the Hare and Hounds Inn, located in the village of

Westridge. The fabled Danny-in-the-Dales area lay a few miles away from the Inn, west of Squire Broadlands' estate.

One Saturday morning in May, the dawn appeared hazy and warm, as if it were reluctant to shake off its quiet slumber. Mr McSwindle rubbed his hands together as the first few ticket holders walked uncertainly towards the belching Deltic and its consist of condemned carriages.

What made matters somewhat confusing for the less informed was another special train one track over from the 'Deltic Flyer'. This one boasted a mixed traffic engine of Great Western origin with impeccably turned out stock of chocolate and cream. The engine itself was in fine array, as the numerous camera-toting enthusiasts attested. Needless to say, the 'Great Western Special' passengers knew which train was *theirs*.

The blue smoke from its competitor befuddled the truly ignorant as they confoundedly referred to what was up front as a steam engine "because of the smoke". However, this is where Ian pointed the way in a somewhat contemptuous manner.

Once inside the carriages, the six Deltic zealots and the rest found the Mark 1s in deplorable condition. The floors had not been swept, windows refused to open, and all the gangways save one were locked shut. Without the right staff….

The 'Great Western Special' whistled off at 8:00 and pulled out of Paddington station in grand style. Enthusiasts lined the permanent way (with a respectable distance) and innumerable cameras captured the gleaming manifest that spoke of the proud customs of that famous and revered company. The sold-out train quickly gathered speed and in a few moments was out of sight. A rousing cheer went down the line as homage was paid to an example of the Great Tradition.

At 8:14 the Deltic belched, barked, blew water from unexpected places, stalled, and died. 'Old Rust and Rivets' was in no mood to leave the station, and no amount of coaxing and swearing by the BR crew, hired only yesterday, could get it to start. An engine foreman was called by an anxious stationmaster who wanted the 'Flyer' out of his environs as soon as possible.

At 8:49 a very large man in stained overalls and smoking a big cigar was seen striding towards the engine with numerous spanners and tools. An engine driver walking nearby called to him.

"Right, Longspan, that thing take you back?"

Longspan stopped, growled, and turned a fearsome eye towards the driver.

"Time was when steam ruled this place. Then things like these came along. Poor substitutes they was, an—"

"Did ya see that Great Western—"

"I did. A fine consist and engine too. If I had the day off—"

Giving the crew a sardonic glance as he climbed into the cab, Longspan soon set to task. After ten minutes of pounding and banging, as well as an adjustment made to the control stand, the Deltic coughed, sputtered, and started. Then he emerged, sullen and wise. McSwindle peered at him as he hit the platform with both feet square. He gave the following to the crew and McSwindle:

"Now you listen. That engine ain't fit t' pull a guard's van t' where you want t' go." He shook a spanner at the Deltic. McSwindle murmured something about "the trip being paid for".

"Be off wi' you then!" shouted Longspan. "Odds are you'll be rememberin' my words." With that he strode back to the engine shed, shaking his head gravely.

At 9:09, over an hour late, the 'Deltic Flyer' wheezed its way out of Paddington. A grateful stationmaster waved good-bye to the unkempt rake of two carriages. Later, it was discovered that McSwindle was not on board. Rumour has it that he set out for the coast that very morning, making his getaway to Limerick. Or did he?

Two miles out of the station, the engine decided it was carrying too much weight and dropped a piece of the concave roof sheeting on its right side. It crashed to the ground alongside the permanent way with a theatrical spin.

A casual passer-by in a nearby lane saw the metal fall off the right side of the engine and notified BR Police.

Despite the best actions of the crew, the Deltic could only manage 20 miles per hour. This was not lost on the passengers, who attributed the slow speed to the newly invented 'Scenic Route'. The 'attractions' included many blocks of unknown buildings, row houses, and members of Maggie's Army lolling about.

Two hours into the trip, the 'Flyer' had only made 40 miles, and at Milepost 41, 'Old Rust and Rivets' decided to take a rest. After wheezing and emitting two very odd noises, the Deltic belched, barked, blew water from unexpected places, stalled, and died. Then the horn began its unceasing blaring, and nothing the crew did could shut it off.

Of course, all this did not go unnoticed by the passengers. Cries of "We're here!" turned to "We're tellin' 'em t' get outta our way." The DOSE members decided, "Must be a picture stop." So the six members got out of their filthy seats and jumped off the lone open gangway.

"Let's get pictures of our favourite engine!" exclaimed one chubby Deltic admirer. A short walk brought them to the front of the train.

"Here, stand by the pilot," implored one man in a BP cap.

"Here, what happened t' the engine?" asked a fellow named Bob 'Brake' Cuthbert, pointing to the engine.

"Look, it's missin' its right side," answered the chubby man.

"Shut off that horn!" hollered 'Diesel' Dan above the noise.

"It's not running."

"G'way from the pilot!"

"Stop talkin'. I'm recording the engine."

"I told you, it's not runnin'!"

Meanwhile, one of the crew, in sheer desperation, took a large spanner and hit the driver's control stand. The Deltic coughed, sputtered, and started.

"Glory be," said Compter, the driver. "Jackie, you've got the touch, lad."

The Deltic was on its way, stuck horn still blaring and missing six bewildered enthusiasts trackside.

"Where yer goin'?" implored Diesel Dan.

"Sorry, lads; once it's goin' I dare not stop!" shouted the frustrated driver as the train began picking up some speed.

"Now wot? They've left us an' no prospect of gettin' back on," lamented Diesel Dan, one of the six stranded. He peculiarly felt this loss, as he was head of DOSE. And what a sight he was, standing trackside, and watching the 'Flyer' limp along. Dan was about five-feet four, of sallow face and slipshod manner. He looked like he hadn't had a change of clothes in days. His black hair was matted with an unknown substance.

"Oh, shut up, Dan," snapped the chubby man in overalls, waving a pasty hand. "Just get on with you."

"Where, eh?" asked a tall, rangy-looking fellow from Jersey.

"Pick up yer feet an' you'll see where they'll take you," answered the same man, known as 'Deltic Dibble'. The little band of Deltic admirers began moving in single file.

"This brings to mind something akin to a hiking club," commented Ladderman, the man from Jersey.

"And yer hikin' days is over!" The group stopped abruptly as five policemen confronted them. "Hikin' on the tracks? Well, ye'll soon be kilt by the passin' trains."

"Hold on there, Ernest," cautioned the second. "Likely as not they're trespassin'."

"Leave us alone," whined Diesel Dan. "They left us."

"*Who* left yuh, yer mum?" asked Ernest. Then he blew a whistle, and a van pulled up on a nearby lane.

"Ye kin tell it t' the Inspector. In yuh go, then!" commanded Ernest as the constables herded the six into the back of the van. Ernest slammed the doors shut and the van was on its way to the nearest police station.

Inspector Sternli was a large, serious man with a moustache and an unmistakably Victorian air about him. His office was simply furnished, with everything in its proper place. A window was open to allow some of the warm spring air into the stillness. The walls were decorated with commendations and old railway photographs.

Interviewing all six DOSE members was not easy. Furthermore, they had no proof of anything they said: no timetable, handbill, programme, or itinerary – just the half-ripped tickets two riders had bothered to keep.

However, the Inspector soon put an end to any doubts about their stories by telephoning the Paddington stationmaster who verified the existence of the 'Deltic Flyer', and also the delays caused by a wheezing old engine. Once that was done, the Inspector assembled the hapless bunch, explained his findings, and advised them to get on the next train back to London at the closet BR station. This they did, and as the 2:34 pulled out of the station, they dreamed about food or cursed their fate. The reader will be left to judge if theirs was the kinder. From London they dispersed, each to his own special place within the Kingdom. Don 'Oily Oil' Wilson went south to Kent, Deltic Dibble headed back to Newcastle, Bob 'Brake' Cuthbert took off for his native Cornwall, Big Jake O'Flaherity went home to somewhere in Belfast, Ladderman was bound for Jersey, and Dan, well, some awful place in East London, on Pudding Lane. He kept their addresses in a faded old notepad, but the brief history of DOSE must now be put on hold….

'Old Rust and Rivets' was now making 21 miles per hour. Was it Divine Providence or did Jackie Smalls really have the touch?

The 95 still on board were glad the other six had left, for they were not really along for the ride, nor were they true Deltic enthusiasts, or members of DOSE. They had aims of capturing Danny-in-the-Dales, finding his lair, and getting rich.

At Milepost 44, the Deltic belched, barked, blew water from unexpected places, stalled, and died again. Jackie was summoned with his spanner to the driver's control stand. After two hard strikes, the Deltic coughed, sputtered, wheezed, and started. Two miles down the line it was making 25 miles per hour.

By now, the passengers had grown restless and hungry. No

provisions had been made for lunch, so they either dreamed about food, urinated out of the single open gangway, or cursed their fate.

Meanwhile 'Old Rust and Rivets' had dropped a piece of its concave roof sheeting on the left side of the engine; only this time the wind blew it backwards, and it fell on top of the first carriage and remained there, balanced precariously between and above the gangways. Suddenly it crashed to the side of the permanent way, and alarmed the jittery emotions of the more restive patrons.

"Here, the roof's cavin' in!"

"Oh, help, help!"

"Easy now, eezzee."

"Where is Broadlands Halt?"

"We should 'ave been there 'ours ago."

"Where is those bags for the gold sov'rins?"

"Where is the manager?"

"Where is the Hare and Hounds?"

At Milepost 50, the Deltic stalled. This time, no amount of banging by Jackie could bring it to move. Apparently, the regulator was stuck. The Deltic wheezed in place, but did not emit anything else unusual. The crew were in a deep state of depression when a shrill whistle to their right distracted them.

"Here, wot ye stopped for, an' why yer 'orn still blowin'?"

The crew tried to lean out of the cracked glass window at a sight they had not imagined. There, to the right, ran a track which curved into the verdant hills amidst swaying tree branches and birds calling their mates. A 42XX Class steam locomotive with a train of six goods wagons was backing down a siding next to a depot built in the early part of the century. A fireman was seen shovelling coal into the firebox and adjusting a gauge. The engine driver was fixing a strong gaze at the crew, then applied the brakes to his own train.

"Wot's that, a tourist train?" sneered Compter.

"Here, now – this engine's been workin' nigh onto 50 year. 'Ow long did that scrap pile last ye?" chuckled the grizzled driver of the steam engine. He glanced over to his fireman with a wink, who then looked out of his own window and nodded. "We'll see who gets the last laugh today."

After Harding uncoupled the wagons, Steadman whistled off, and moved his engine onto an adjacent track with his fireman working the switches. A BR engine soon had the same wagons underway, bound for London.

"Wot's the train of the past called?" persisted Compter. At that, the grizzled driver left his footplate as Harding swung on, and walked over to the disabled train.

"This ain't no tourist train. This 'ere's the Dormand and Farmington Railway."

A short aside to the reader may be of help. The area has long been known for the raising of the excellent quality of pork, and a railway was built in the 1880s to help carry it and the high quality of farm products to the mainline. Today, the Dormand and Farmington continues in private ownership and prosperity.

At this point, two old and large touring cars, which happened to be rounding a bend in a nearby road, stopped rather abruptly. A group of gentlemen, clad in their Sunday best (though it wasn't Sunday), hurried themselves down a slight hill to catch more than a glance at the Dormand and Farmington's engine No 1.

"Bless my soul, I think I'm in my prime again!" exclaimed Mr Bagnall.

"Methinks I'm reliving my better days," reflected Mr Hudswell Clarke.

"I'm getting up there to check her," pronounced Mr Hawthorn-Leslie. He was followed by Messrs Austerity, Manning Wardle, Hewley Mills, Peckett, and Hunslet. Harding graciously alighted to give the men more room on the footplate.

Mr Manning Wardle, having inspected the footplate and gauges, said, "Not enough water in the glass," whereupon Mr Hewley Mills told everyone he agreed.

"Not so. There's plenty of water," groused Mr Hawthorn-Leslie.

"Quite right," said Mr Austerity gravely.

An argument ensued as to whether the fire was properly banked or not, the fire burning correctly, the coal good quality, the water too high or low (again), the engine too dirty, the brake handle too loose, the regulator too tight, the lamps displayed properly.

Suddenly, Mr Peckett moved towards a suspended handle. "Methinks a tug'll stop this harangue," and with that, the shrillness of Engine No 1's whistle rendered the arguments moot.

Jackie had chosen this moment to put an end to the horn by locating and cutting the wire as well. A strange silence fell over the tracks.

The Dormand's driver, having been severely startled by the sound of his own whistle, turned quickly back towards his engine.

"An' wot yer doin' up there on my footplate!" he yelled, whereupon all the previous arguments began. He motioned Harding to follow him.

"G'way from the engine!" shouted the grizzled veteran as he lunged the coal scoop menacingly at the group. This had the effect of scattering the men off No 1 and they moved a safe distance away from the track. They wearily made their way to the depot's platform and consulted themselves as to what their next move would be.

"Let's get back on her anyway," Mr Hunslet said. "He'll be driving her back soon, and I happen to know it's a good 15 miles to the end of the line."

"And what about the cars, eh?" asked Mr Peckett.

"It's too long a walk for us to get back here," reminded Mr Hewley Mills.

"And how do you propose to get us back?" queried Mr Austerity, in a grave manner.

After another argument, Mr Hudswell Clarke solved the situation by telling his friends, "Let us be on our way to Line's End, observe this splendid engine returning to its home depot, and plan our next trip for tomorrow over supper."

"If we can get there before he does," sighed Mr Hawthorn Leslie. "Come on then. The driver has his job to do." They took pictures of the engine, the depot, and the junction, but not the 'Flyer'. They then made their way back to the cars, and, casting wistful glances at the Dormand and Farmington's No 1, reluctantly left the scene.

A diesel horn interrupted this time, but not from the seemingly immovable Deltic. A goods train had been creeping on a red signal towards the 'Flyer', and stopped a respectable distance away. The goods driver blasted the stalled train again and again with his horn. This caused Steadman to laugh as Harding threw another scoopful of coal into the fire. "*Modern* technology, they call it."

The goods driver, having climbed down from his engine, strode towards the Deltic. The hapless crew hit the ballast as they sensed a row. Some passengers left the coaches and surrounded the would-be combatants, or so they hoped.

"Get that thing going. Yer holdin' me up," said the goods driver.

"I can't. Regulator's stuck," said Compter as the engine continued to idle.

"I happen t' know there's three behind me. Now wot d'ya say t'that?" asked the goods driver, his voice rising.

Our grizzled friend, having observed the happenings, and having taught the elder gents that a respectable distance from Harding's coal scoop was warranted, entered the scene.

"'E may need the Dormand yet."

"Wot's that? The Dormand? How could you do anything?" asked Compter sarcastically.

"Wot kin that line do for us?" Jackie had his doubts as well.

"Well, there's a siding by Broadlands Halt. That be about seven mile. No, I'll haul ya there, but I reckon you'll need permission first."

"Yer daft. That old engine o' yours couldn't move us anywhere," grumbled Compter.

"How far izzit from the Hare and Hounds?" queried one of the passengers, a man in a brown suit.

"At this rate we might never get there," sighed another passenger.

"I'll call ahead and see if the old man can park yer arse on that siding," offered the goods driver. Five minutes later he was back with an affirmative.

"Can't be done," countered Compter. "Old Grizzly is dreamin' if he thinks his engine can move this train at all."

"Well, wot's yer alternative?" protested the goods driver. Silence. "Then I say let 'im have a go."

Pluckworth, having reversed his train enough for Steadman, backed a bit further for good measure. With Harding at the switch, the steam engine cleared the points, then coupled onto the disabled train. Steadman whistled off, Compter released the brakes, and our grizzled friend reversed, then began pushing as the 'Flyer' entered the Dormand and Farmington Railway. Harding secured the switch and swung on as Steadman momentarily paused for him. Pushing the formerly stalled train was no hardship whatsoever. Pluckworth, having helped to orchestrate this scenario, was soon on his way as well.

In what seemed to be a matter of a few minutes, the train had slowed to a stop. A switch was thrown, and the 43XX pushed the disabled train onto Broadlands Halt siding. After securing the 'Flyer', a reverse move by Steadman, lining up to points, and locking the switch, Harding swung on. Steadman acknowledged the grateful waves of the Deltic crew and its more informed passengers. He and his mate had quite a story to tell friends that night.

Broadlands Halt was a country station in the truest sense of the word. It being Saturday, the stationmaster was not on duty. The passengers clambered out of the lone open gangway, scarcely able to wait their turn. They all stood on the platform, waiting expectantly.

"Where, where is it?" asked someone. 'It' was the 'bus, or small fleet of 'busses, that was supposed to convey them to the Hare and Hounds for supper, a night's lodging, and a speculative venture the following morning. A half day had been allotted for the get-rich-quick scheme. But McSwindle had forgotten (or failed) to charter anything. Besides, where was one going to find 'busses out there?

Jackie, having grown up there and retaining some knowledge of the area, advised the passengers that Broadlands Halt was a good five miles from the Hare and Hounds.

The same brown-suited man suggested calling the local taxi

service, if there was one. The number was procured from Jackie, and the one telephone at the station soon became a point of interest. Mr Brown Suit made the call himself. "We have reservations at the Hare and Hounds. Come get us immediately," telephoned the earnest gold-seeker.

Wynn, the local taxi driver, had his doubts when he drove up to the station and saw an ill-clad crowd milling about. Were *these* people attending the Ball?

"Right. Four at a time," announced Wynn. "Three pound per person—"

"How kin you take alla us in that thing?"

"Three pounds! You dirty, cheating—"

"Louse!"

"Thief!"

"Footpad!"

"Scoundrel!"

"Right – then you 'ave a pleasant walk!" shouted Wynn. No amount of coaxing or pleading could persuade him to change his mind, for Wynn had a stubborn streak. Besides, there was plenty of business lined up for the evening. Not everyone who was invited to the Spring Ball was driving. Having recognized Jackie, however, he did consent to take him and Compter into the village for a few quid.

While some elected to "wait for the 'bus", most of the aspiring rich took to the country lane that led to the village of Westridge. They watched ruefully as the taxi gradually began to disappear in front of them. More than a few had to turn back because of cheap shoes.

Five hours later, the motley assemblage straggled into the village. They were met by curious glances from the village folk and passers-by. When the Hare and Hounds was found and reached, they proceeded en masse through a side door, the main one too crowded with the comings and goings of the Spring Ball preparation.

"We're here!" yelled one.

"Where's my room?" asked another.

"I'm hungry!" shouted a dishevelled man of five and thirty.

"Where's my room?" mumbled a tired treasure-hunter-to-be.

"What do you mean, 'Where's my room?' 'We're here!'; Who are you?" The receptionist was somewhat taken aback.

"You know. We're on the 'Flyer.' We're here t' find Danny-in-the-Dales,' explained a sprightly woman.

Dead silence.

"We have reservations," said Mr Brown Suit confidently.

The receptionist found words, after a minute of this. "I'm afraid you're mistaken. We have no reservations for anyone except for the Spring Ball, which is scheduled for this evening. We have no extra rooms available."

"Well, then where is McSwindle? He said he'd arrange lodging for us and the Danny search," whined a forlorn-looking short man with a tartan shirt.

"Give us our rooms. Now!"

"Show us the loos. An' be quick about it!"

"Hiked 50 miles to get here!" This was a deliberate exaggeration, used to try and win some sympathy.

"I say, who are these people?" A member of the local gentry had entered the foyer, followed by several other gentlemen. The receptionist explained the 'situation'. Then this same gentleman turned to the restive, angry crowd, indicated someone standing nearby, and advised:

"This is Squire Broadlands. He can try and help you—"

"We don't need no help!"

"Where are the bags for the sov'rins?"

"Gimme my room!"

"Right, an' be quick about it."

"Where's the loo? Now!"

"Oy, when's supper?"

"I don' see no Wimpy Bar round 'ere. How do you expect us t' survive?"

"Here, let's just push an' shove these country dolts around. That'll get 'em t' listen t' us. Ready? One, two—"

"Throw this rabble out!" exclaimed an older gentleman. "This will never do." And so the motley assemblage was pushed out of the Inn and directed back the way they had come.

They found a small plot of land halfway through the village to make a temporary encampment. Here they fell to earth, hungry, thirsty, angry, and dispirited. Some decided to relieve themselves behind the clumps of higher bushes, while the others sank in dejection.

Several enterprising merchants, having spotted the bunch of interlopers, soon were peddling food and drinks at rather high prices. Spirits revived, their stomachs halfway full, or more, but news of no lodging only made them angrier. A few empty bottles were hurled in the general direction of the Hare and Hounds. The merchants had already drifted back to their shops, counting the cash with some glee.

"Here, where's that McSwindle?"

"Do ya think he pocketed the cash?"

"I dunno. Now what to do?"

"Where are we going? What are we doing… now?"

"Where's the bags for the sov'rins?"

It was now wearing on to an early evening. No one was willing to assume any leadership (not even Mr Brown Suit), and the result was nothing but internal chaos. After finishing their expensive suppers, little groups of people broke off from the main crowd, wandering aimlessly into the surrounding country. Some of the more focused passengers, about 20, decided to walk back to the station to "wait for the 'bus". Along the way, they stopped at the local spirits shoppe and hastily purchased beer and liquors for the needed fortification which lay ahead. Extra bottles were bought in anticipation of the needs of those who were still waiting at Broadlands Halt. The purchasers concluded that profits could easily be made, and they were, somewhat later. The rest had departed the village by the time they started back, ranging around to all points of the compass.

Meanwhile, Jackie decided to look up a friend who proved willing to provide food, drink, and lodging for him and his mate. "We'll telephone London in the morning," said Compter. But Jackie, in a fit of conscience, made the call after the first round at the local pub.

A band of disoriented treasure-seekers, having wandered off the dim outline of a country lane they were attempting to follow, had mistakenly entered the land belonging to Squire Broadlands. The good Squire's able ward, a Mr Sharp, was making his final rounds on horseback and confronted them.

"State yer business."

"We're looking for—"

"We're trying to find Danny-in-the-Dales an'—"

"Yer trespassin.' This is Squire Broadlands' estate."

As Mr Sharp was speaking, shadowy figures loomed behind tall rushes and trees in a section of the estate referred to as The Red Woods. The workmen were returning from their day's labours, carrying their rakes and shovels. However, the illusionary nature they displayed in the waning light gave them a menacing quality as they advanced towards the hapless vagabonds.

"Clear out. Follow that fence down t' the road and be on yer way!"

They bolted as one and ran pell-mell along the fence. They kept running once they reached the road. Little did they realize that their opportunity would soon be upon them.

After a good half mile they turned, and perceiving that they were not being pursued, slowed down to a walk. This they continued for some time, until one of them suggested they rest at the bottom of a pleasant, grassy hill to their left. This was agreed to, and soon everyone was hunting for a good place to assuage the long and unexpected hours spent in walking. Most chose to lie down under the trees nearby, although Mr Brown Suit picked some soft grass a little farther away. With a collective sigh, they all collapsed, noting the warm and soothing breeze that stirred the branches above them.

Thus they dozed, not knowing of the full moon that was rising to their left. The moon passed over the trees slowly and then became seemingly positioned over a large hill above them.

At that instant, a small elfish creature appeared, dancing, turning somersaults, skipping, singing, and laughing. The magical hour had arrived, and our fortune-seekers were oblivious to it!

Eventually Mr Brown Suit, sleeping on the soft grass, was awakened abruptly by a nightmare in which he had crashed the Deltic engine into the end of a siding. He rubbed his eyes and looked round to make certain he had not really done it! Then his left eye caught the little figure on the hill, clad in green, dancing and skipping to his heart's content.

"I say! It's what we've come for! It's Danny-in-the-Dales! Wake up, I say, wake up!"

Rousing his comrades was not easy, but once they saw Danny on top of that hill, dancing and singing in the splendour of a full moon, they sprang to their feet and half ran up that same hill, yelling, "We've found him!"

Danny did not appear to take notice of his adversaries, and continued his frolics, albeit a few rods away from where he began. As the group neared the top of the hill, he began moving slowly away, dancing and capering, but he stopped singing. The boyish figure with the generous smile leaped through some rocks and was off, descending the hill through a stand of elms.

While he drew them farther and farther away from the pleasant area where they had rested, they found it increasingly difficult to keep up with him. At first, this did not alarm them, but soon they were in the dales, where the moonlight had trouble reaching them.

Danny paused under a huge elm and considered his foe. They were facing someone with an infinite knowledge of the realm which he called his own. Down one hill, up another, down, into the dales they were, and still they followed. He merely noted their tired attempts to keep up and was off again, skipping and leaping over rocks and rills.

Soon Danny disappeared into another dale, his green outfit unrecognizable in the dense growth beneath the towering elms. Once the group realized they had lost him, they stopped to rest. Where were they? Somewhere in a dark dell with no clear trail – but that was all they knew.

Suddenly, someone shouted, "Look, there he is!" On top of the next hill, dancing and smiling, was Danny-in-the-Dales. He was too far away from them this time, but no one was willing to admit it.

"Come on. Those sov'rins'll be ours if we catch him!" yelled a young man in black trousers and mauve shirt. His rousing call-to-riches got the rest on their feet. Upon reaching the top of the hill they discovered Danny had gone and the moon was no longer seemingly fixed in its former position. They tramped on, up and down several more hills, then found themselves in a dell so dark they could scarcely see any moonlight at all.

After several minutes of wandering, they reached the foot of another hill – only this time, they saw an opening of a damp cave. Cool, dank air refreshed their sweaty bodies as they paused to marvel at their discovery. This instantly cheered them up, figuring they had, at long last, found *the* place where Danny was really keeping those 20 or so pots of gold sovereigns. They yelled and stamped their feet in the excitement of the moment. Then, without another thought, they plunged headlong into the interminable darkness, becoming separated and losing their way all within the span of several minutes. Did they expect the way to be lit for them? No one had thought about a possible need for torches....

Their subsequent cries of anguish diminished as they stumbled further and further into the caverns and twisted passageways known only to a few of the local yeoman as The Maze. It was generally considered too dangerous to attempt an exploration. Only Danny himself knew where all the trails in The Maze led, and he rarely used it except under uncommon circumstances. Although it had been a few years since anyone had really tried to catch him, tonight was not one of those times when he elected to enter The Maze.

He had eluded them as he had eluded others before. He continued dancing and skipping until the moon became lost in some clouds which came up over the hills without warning. Then he suddenly vanished in the depths of a valley, not to appear again that night.

Unfortunately, we must now leave our lost and helpless treasure-hunters, since having plunged into the nether regions of The Maze, they became hopelessly confounded, and were never heard of or seen again.

Those enterprising gold-seekers who had settled on making the trip back to Broadlands Halt were met with derision by those who had elected to stay. Arguments raged back and forth while fruitless efforts to extract more candy from the now empty candy machine were jeered at by others who had hoarded what remained at an earlier hour. The weary ones did find a water fountain at the end of the platform, next to a thick, high-sided wooden fence with spear-like ends facing the heavens.

Then, at a predetermined signal, bottles suddenly appeared in front of the jeering 'bus waiters. Desperate for any remission from the travails which had been inflicted upon them, they eagerly purchased the beer and spirits (at inflated prices), quaffed their newly found friends, and were temporarily satisfied.

The more easily frightened members of the exploratory division thought that, for security purposes, they should best board the train and wait out their rescue. Their counterparts, who decided to spend their time on the platform, hooted and slandered them as they made themselves as comfortable as they could in the Mark 1s. There they swilled their own liquids, silently enjoying the effect of too much alcohol against too little food. Once everything was consumed, and the effects began to catch up with our weary explorers, the stillness of a country station and the coolness of a lovely country evening eventually had all sound asleep, each at his or her own special time.

While those who slept at Broadlands Halt dreamt of shiny gold sovereigns, food, or subconsciously cursed their fate, an angry crew in a Bobo Diesel were making their way to the little station, arrangements having been made earlier.

"Special! Special excurrrssionn! Well, damn 'em all!" The BR driver was put out, even though he was getting paid extra for it. "Why we booked on for this—"

"You know, Smithson wouldn't've 'ad us out 'ere 'less it was some emergency," reminded his mate. "After all them breaks we got… time we did somethin' for him."

"'Deltic Flyer', Deltic in the fire! Longspan warned 'em not t' make the trip. An' wot d' they do? Go anyway! Ex-currrsion, bah! Read the orders again!"

"Says t'pick up the carriages an' bring 'em back t' Paddington. But no mention of the engine. Why d'ya suppose that is?" asked his mate.

"I 'eard they was callin' that thing 'Old Rust and Rivets'," roared the driver, ignoring the question. "An' they found a piece of it not five mile from the station."

"Why d'ya think they left off the engine?" persisted his mate.

"Maybe they wanna sacrifice it in one of them crackpot *notions* some o' these louts 'ave," snickered the driver.

"Still, seems kind o' odd."

The siding was reached in night's early hours. As Sedge uncoupled the carriages from the crippled engine, he noticed a large group of people sleeping deeply on the platform. He hurried up to the cab and whispered, "Say, Chalky, what d'ya make o' that?" He pointed towards the platform.

Chalky leaned out the window and observed the snoring mass. "Hmmm… must be vagrants. We better give BR a call."

"Right," whispered Sedge. "Should we wake them up?"

"What for?"

Five minutes later, the Bobo and carriages were on their way back to Paddington. So deep was their slumber that those who slept onboard as well as those left at Broadlands Halt knew nothing of recent developments, save one. Upon awakening and feeling the moving train, he reasoned that he was still dreaming, and drifted back to Gold Sovereign Land.

Upon arriving in London, Chalky was directed to leave the carriages on a special track in the marshalling yard. There they were to be cleaned and sold (or rented) to another aspiring enthusiast group. Chalky's rather abrupt application of the brakes jarred the carriages, causing their inhabitants a somewhat rude awakening. When the train came to its final stop, everyone was fully awake but literally thrown into confusion. All the noise emanating from the carriages caught the ears of Chalky's mate as he was walking past the rake. He hurried back to the cab.

"Say, Chalky, there's people in them carriages, there is!"

"Wot? Then call BR Police."

Before those on board knew what was happening, a dozen policemen had gained access to the carriages. All were arrested and packed off to jail. The excursionists were too tired to plead their cases.

At dawn's early light, regional BR Police surrounded the 'vagrants' at Broadlands Halt and promptly arrested them for trespassing. The 'vagrants', being the feistier bunch, offered some feeble resistance, which was duly noted by the chief constable.

That same morning, a call was put into Line's End to the Dormand and Farmington Railway. The office being closed, the call was routed to Steadman's house. Would he and his mate bring the Deltic back to Paddington, seeing as how the orders Chalky received were incomplete? Coal and water would be provided, of course. After a generous sum was proffered, he agreed, called Harding, and they began making their preparations.

Somehow the word had gotten out to enthusiasts, and dozens lined the permanent way, waving, shouting their approval, and snapping photographs. The number grew as Steadman and Harding conveyed the Deltic closer and closer to London.

Upon arrival, they were greeted as celebrities. The stationmaster shook their hands, enthusiasts gave them a rousing cheer, and their picture with No 1 and the story made the Monday morning edition of *The Daily Telegraph.*

"I told that bloke we'd see who'd 'ave the last laugh," Steadman was quoted as saying. The ride back to Line's End was just as triumphant.

The BR crew at Westridge were told to catch the 1:03 to London. A disheartened spell fell over them as they recalled Longspan's words while boarding the train.

And those who had wandered away from the village in all directions? They are still wandering aimlessly about for all I know. Wouldn't you? After all, wouldn't you like to find 20 pots full of gold sovereigns?

## CHAPTER TWO
# The Five O'Clock Surprise

It being Tuesday night, the Second Street Railway Enthusiasts Club were gathered in their dimly lit meeting hall. The hall itself once housed a debating society during the heyday of Fabian persuasion. Now its existence depended upon the modest sums collected by the proprietor, who was reportedly known for his fondness of Cuban cigars.

Cigar, pipe, and cigarette smoke eddied around the porcelain light fixtures as the hall buzzed with the animated conversations of its temporary dwellers. A large yellow stripe was painted down the middle of the once bright wooden floor, separating row upon row of men seated in folding chairs. On the left sat the 'Bobos' (four-axled diesel enthusiasts), and on the right sat the 'Cocos' (six-axled diesel enthusiasts). The Bobos wore grey and the Cocos wore brown. Those of the steam persuasion were interspersed on both sides. Of course, the inevitable arguments raged back and forth across the demilitarized zone, sometimes good-natured, or otherwise:

"We're faster 'n' you!"

"Eh? We can pull more!"

"We're more versatile!"

"Try pullin' all them coal wagons! Ya can't!"

"Wot's used on expresses?"

The steam men were silent, allowing the arguments to go on without their own comments. Then, just before the meeting was called, there began a cry in antiphonal fashion:

"Bobos!"

"Cocos!"

"Bobos!"

"Cocos!"

The level of noise rose until the sound was deafening. Then a Bobo crossed the yellow line which caused an instantaneous reaction by the Cocos, and the result was he was thrown back to his compatriots. Other Bobos took up the offensive, but the Cocos rose as one and successfully repelled the intruders with aplomb. The Bobos, defeated yet again, took their seats dejectedly, cursing their fate and foe, until 'Bobo Bic' Narclay called the meeting to order.

"Right, an' I see you've been at it again. Really, must all our meetings start in such a manner?"

"The sewin' circle meets here tomorrow," snickered a Coco.

"Right, and 'ow do you know that?" asked a short-statured Bobo. The Bobos tittered in response. Cocos fumed threateningly.

After Old Business was dealt with and New Business begun, a little bespectacled man in a loud tweed suit approached the speaker's platform with a handbill.

"Good evening, good evening. I have asked the Chair to speak on something which I believe you will find most enlightening, enjoyable, fun, educational, historically accurate, authentic, and true to form. I am here tonight, representing the Korkerhill and Spaniel Downss (Preserved) Railway—"

"Never heard of it."

"Oh, come come. Surely you have heard of this very famous line which played an extremely important part in saving the renowned Count Okropoli-Simkovitch in the Great War—"

"Eh?" Old Dickerson was having trouble hearing again. His right ear "came and went", in his words. He usually sat in a front row, but that didn't always help.

The bespectacled man continued. "Well, the historical fact is that if it weren't for the Korkerhill and Spaniel Downss (Preserved) Railway—"

"We'd all be 'ome now, we would," interjected a Bobo.

"I say, you certainly are a rude bunch, aren't you? That's the third time I have been interrupted!"

Murmurs of disapproval began instantly. Then a voice from the middle of the room rang out: "Are you a Bobo or a Coco?"

"I beg your pardon?" Bookley did not know what to make of this strange challenge.

"Oh, get on with it," sighed the treasurer.

"Well, since you men are obviously in a state of anxiety, owing to your own filthy lifestyles, while I rest easily on my own pillars, I will (regretfully) shorten this very worthwhile presentation of facts to mention just a few words concerning the Count Okropoli-Simkovitch and how the Korkerhill and Spaniel Downss Railway, intrepid builders, visionaries, luminaries, endowed with too many talents, models for the time in which they stood, examples to future peoples, and that greatest of men, one Grant Overbuild, who sneered at Brunel, who by his own dedication and great gifts of many years ago, achieved—"

"What gibberish. Where did they ever get this fellow?" complained the elder Smythe-Jones.

"This fellow prates on and on," agreed Mr Readily.

"Oh, I say, and say again, refrain from these awful interruptions," bewailed Bookley. "I say, and say again, that the good Count would never have made his getaway on November 15, 1917, if it weren't for the Korkerhill and Spaniel Downss Railway, this important man may not have ever gotten away, and he enjoyed his secret ride in the private saloon for which he paid 100 guineas, just to ride in it, not the usual carriages, but he could have ridden in one of the other carriages, in a secret disguise—"

"Enough," counselled Bobo Bic.

"Oh, get on with it," sighed the treasurer again.

"Oh, come come! I'm educating these ignorant people—"

"Wot are you doin' here?" challenged a Coco.

"Have you yet to figure it out? I am here representing the Korkerhill and Spaniel Downss (Preserved) Railway because of our historical importance in the Great War, involving secret negotiations with Czar Nicholas II's government by the great Count Okropoli-Simkovitch—"

Men began to get up on both sides of the aisles and leave in protest. Bookley, seeing that he was literally losing his audience, hastily changed his tactics.

“I say, gentlemen (?), will you all quickly retake your seats, for I have some startling news to tell you.” Collective groans and sighs gave way to silence. They were going to give him one last chance.

“I say—”

“You say too much!” growled a burly Coco.

“Really? I have barely gotten started.” (Groans.) Bookley turned away from the microphone briefly and was heard by a few to remark: “Pigs. That’s what we have here.” Then he spoke into the microphone for all to hear. “But I see you are anxious… so… my purpose of coming here tonight, besides to educate you… is to inform you that the Korkerhill and Spaniel Downss (Preserved) Railway is pleased to offer you, the Third Street Railway—”

“That’s Second Street, you blighter!” yelled a Bobo.

“Well! Ah… we are offering… the Club… an ‘Enthusiasts Afternoon’ along with a few other invited Clubs. It is going to be complete with an informative lecture, by me, of course; period carriages, the Count, our Food Hut, Souvenir Shop, engine shed, and a big surprise.”

“Wot izzit?”

“Oh, you *children*! Do you really expect me to reveal that?”

“No, we really don’t,” countered the exasperated treasurer. “Now give us the date and time, please.”

“I’d like for the Club to see that for themselves,” answered Bookley with a sniff. “Ian!” He motioned towards a figure lurking in the shadows of an exit door. “Pass out the handbills.”

A man of middling height, dark curly hair, wearing a bottle green Tyrolean hat, tattersall vest, and a Black Watch suit began nervously distributing handbills with the day’s itinerary on them. Once the schedules were in hand, Ian approached the platform, his eyes darting back and forth across the hall, as if he were looking for someone, or, something.

Bookley made some joke to himself, then spoke into the

microphone again. "This is Ian McSwindle. He has generously offered to arrange the entire trip to the Korkerhill and Spaniel Downss (Preserved) Railway for you, including the chartering of some 'Jumbo Tour' 'busses from Blue-Ped-on-Riveredge Station to our wonderful Railway."

A lanky Bobo stood up. "'Generous', is he? Here, lads, he's the one who got those blokes in DOSE (all six of them) in trouble."

"You mean those Deltic lads? Yes, I read about that in *The Daily Telegraph*," said the elder Smythe-Jones.

"Right, who doesn't know about that?" retorted another Bobo.

McSwindle began slinking off the platform to the left, apparently heading….

"Come on, lads, let's rush him!" yelled a Coco. McSwindle leaped off the dais, flew out of the left Exit door, and ran for his life down a darkened alley, dodging dustbins the entire way. A score of Bobos and Cocos took off in pursuit, but after several minutes they returned, saying that he had gotten away.

By now the Club members were in an ugly mood. Bic took the microphone away from Bookley and spoke to the restless crowd.

"The sooner we all settle down—"

"I'll tell you what we're going ta settle. We're gonna run this windbag out the bloody door!" yelled a Coco. Many on both sides shouted their approval. The crowd began to advance towards the dais. Bookley grabbed the microphone in desperation.

"Oh, er, gentlemen, we will let you come to the railway and spend the entire afternoon for only 25 pounds—"

"The Devil will pay that sum before I do!"

"Tw-twenty-two pounds," offered Bookley.

"Twenty-two pence!" shouted a few Bobos. The cheer was taken up by the entire Club.

"Twenty-two pence! Twenty-two pence! Twenty-two pence!"

As the men came closer and closer, Bookley realized his life would be decided in a matter of seconds. He held up his sweaty hands in acquiescence. "Very well. Twenty-two pence. I don't know how I am going to explain this to my Board of Directors."

"Tell 'em all yer friends are comin'," sneered an older man.

Bookley vanished in a few seconds. It was later rumoured that the secretary had had him smuggled out the back door. With Bookley gone, New Business was concluded and the meeting was adjourned. The time stood at eleven minutes after nine.

Having made all the arrangements without the 'generosity' of McSwindle, the Club members awaited their bargain basement trip to the Korkerhill and Spaniel Downss (Preserved) Railway. Cameras were loaded, recorders cued, hats and jackets were located and set out the night before. However, no one could find anything in the local library about where they were going. Actually, one had to live in the area to really know the details. It was one of *those* places.

At last, the aforesaid date arrived! Paddington was hushed and shrouded by an early morning fog. The stillness mirrored a timelessness about the weather – forever cool and damp on an early sunless, late spring morning. The lack of activity only served to reinforce the quiet atmosphere. It was in this state that a crew made their way towards a Bobo Diesel. Having received their orders, they climbed up into the cab, coupled onto a short rake of cleaned and serviced Mark 1s, and backed down Track 1. Once the end of the platform was reached, the driver lit a cigar with a wooden match and carelessly tossed it out his window.

"T' think I'm usin' me day off for Smithson like this again," he grumbled. "Another damn excurrrzzhun. That's the curse o' once bein' a top link driver. It's got its good points, but not on days like today. Been a goods driver for years, an' like it, too."

His mate had heard this many times before, so he just let Chalky air his grievances out. "So where we headed?"

"Blue-Ped-on-Riveredge," answered Chalky. "Seems these louts want to go to one o' them preeserved railways."

"Wait… I think I know which one it is," stated Sedge confidently. "It's the Korkerhill and Spaniel Downss (Preserved) Railway."

"Right, an' I live on German Shepherd's Arse Lane," scoffed

Chalky.

"No, really, me mum's from up that way. Some Russian escaped from Red agents on that line back in the Great War."

"Is *that* their claim t' fame? An' wot be that line Old Grizzly works for? You remember them lads tellin' us how he got 'em off the permanent way and such."

"I surely do remember. That were the… Dormand And Farmington. Say, Chalky, how 'bout lettin' me 'ave a go with the engine…."

"Not this again." Chalky shifted in his seat and paused. "Well… maybe."

"Right, an' I'll get your fish an' chips the next time, I will." Sedge then glanced backwards and noted the steady stream of Second Street Railway Enthusiasts moving towards the waiting train.

"Tom's let the gate open… an' 'ere they come!"

Chalky leaned out the window. "Hello, these louts is mostly dressed in grey or brown. I told you some time ago they're all bloody crazy."

A few blasts from the horn only made them move faster to get on board. Chalky began blowing short little blasts, enjoying the effects immensely. "See the little chickens, look how they run," he laughed.

"Say, Chalky, let me 'ave a go," pleaded Sedge.

"Oh, awl riiight," said Chalky resignedly. Sedge gave a long blast which gave the permanent way gang an excuse to scratch their heads. This was followed by a longer blast. After 15 seconds, the horn was still blowing.

"Here, let the damn thing go!" admonished Chalky.

Sedge quietly sat down, smiling and listening to the last echoes bounce off the blackened walls of the overpass.

Meanwhile, the carriages were filling up fast. Few members of the Club were willing to pass up such a bargain as 22 pence for an afternoon outing at a preserved railway. As the grey- and brown-clad men entered each carriage, they instantly separated themselves, although there was no yellow line painted down the middle of each carriage. The grey-clad men sat on the left, and the brown-clad men sat on the right, just as in their meetings. Those who were steam men scattered themselves on both sides. They wore no particular colour, although most had greasecaps with the various badges of the Big Four. Southern and Great Western badges dominated.

A faulty loudspeaker system had been rigged throughout the train the night before by members Jae and Javits, two antique dealers who lived a stone's throw away from where the Club met on Tuesday nights. A clammy, muffled voice was attempting to instruct all who could listen to quickly take their seats so the train could get underway. After clearing his scratchy throat over and over, and spitting out the nearest gangway, Prompter began giving out some 'Dos and Don'ts'.

"Uhh (cough), all Cclubb members sh-should t-take their sseats... now? And r-remammber, whether we b-be Bobos, Cocos, or steam mmen, let's have a s-safe trip, and no rows. Remember the papers you signed? Remember, no leaning out of windows or gangways, no chewing, no spitting (silence)… no hitting, no fighting, no cursing. Be friendly to the other enthusiasts at the Korkerhill. We are all good people… l-let others s-see that! Show your fellow enthusiasts that we can behave as well as any other club out th-there."

A few minutes passed; then Chalky whistled off, and the Second Street Railway Enthusiasts were off to their destination. As the train began to pick up speed, Sedge wondered (a) if he would get another chance to blow the horn, or (b) really have a turn at running the engine, all by himself. What he didn't know was that Fate was weighing his future and career, and, having decided which way events would go, left him alone. Chalky, on the other hand, having weathered the vicissitudes of life a little longer than his mate, was not even considered.

The next meeting of the DOSE Society was held in the back of a dimly lit pub in London near the vicinity of some local scrap yards. This meeting was held in conjunction with a week-long holiday arranged by all its members. Diesel Dan and his unhappy Club members were worried. The recent protests against the impending scrapping of 'Old Rust and Rivets' (called that by BR crews who had the unfortunate job of actually running the engine) had not done a farthing's good to help stop what was apparently an official decision. They had carried signs up and down the restricted area beyond the gates of Bonehead Scrappers, waving down motorists and passers-by to enlist them in their appeal to save the rusting hulk from oblivion. So far only nine pounds had been raised, with 16 signatures on a poorly worded petition. Signs, marches, and watches (two were all night), an appeal, and petition failed to deter what looked like was inevitable. Something had to be done… but what?

Then Bob 'Brake' Cuthbert, a grim-faced man of 40, burst in the door with an urgent message. Bonehead Scrappers were short of workers and had applied to the MSC that very morning. The members voted unanimously to make applications!

But Diesel Dan, Chair of the Club, had much more to think about. He and his Club had to come up with a systematic plan NOT to scrap the engine, but save it. The members entertained proposal after proposal for hours. Then at 12 a.m., the six approved what was later termed "a hare-brained scheme" by Don 'Oily Oil' Wilson. However, it had sounded good at the time, reinforced with fish, chips, and ale. Their raucous approbation quickly became the talk of the other patrons, and they were shown the door soon afterwards with curses by the surly owner.

The next day, six sleepy-eyed men applied for work through the MSC and were directed to Bonehead Scrappers, after each one said they had "experience with metals, scrap, and such". They were told to report to work the following morning, at 8:00. That, incidentally, was the same day of the Second Street Railway Enthusiasts' excursion to the Korkerhill and Spaniel Downss (Preserved) Railway.

So, a day later, they approached the fence by Bonehead Scrappers, Diesel Dan leading the way. An old watchman curiously took in the motley-looking lot. "Here, who might you be?"

"We come t' work," announced Deltic Dibble, a chubby man in overalls.

"Wot them totes for?" asked the watchman, looking at the group from man to man.

"Well, we got t' eat something," answered Ladderman. The watchman nodded in assent.

"Aye. The foreman left these instructions. Now 'e wants you t' start with that rusty hulk on that track there." He pointed to the Deltic, which was parked on a short side track. "'E aims t' get every pound out o' that thing—"

"Here, wot you calling it that 'thing' for? It is a fine engine," said Ladderman.

"Hoot man, be ye daft?" laughed the old Scot. A quick glance by Dan silenced any answer to the contrary. "Now get t' work. 'E said t' start with the externals, of course. You'll find all the tools an' torches you'll need in that shed." With that the DOSE members quickly set to work, tools and torches in hand from the aforementioned shed.

"Oh, what luck," chuckled Dan as he began working on removing the builder's plate.

"This number'll look great over me fireplace," grinned Bob 'Brake' Cuthbert.

"An' this lamp'll suit my porch well," chortled Big Jake O'Flaherity, who lived up to his name in stature and comportment.

"Sure, an' it's all a temporary safeguard 'til we get her running again," cautioned Dan.

The coveted pieces never made it to the ground, or the scrap wagon parked on the next track. They began to mysteriously disappear into the canvas 'lunch' totes brought along expressly for that purpose.

The foreman appeared about an hour later and enquired as to the workings of the newly hired. "Oh, they been at it a while," assured the watchman. As the foreman strolled over to the engine, he noticed that not only were such things as lamps, the horn, number indicator, etc. off the engine, they were not in the scrap wagon, nor on the ground anywhere.

"Here, workin' hard or hardly workin'?" asked Jobson. "Wot you been up to, eh? Where them externals and such?"

"Near as we can figure, vandals be takin' that stuff," said Oily Oil.

"Oh, shut it off," countered Jobson. "Wot you been doin' for an hour?"

"We were inspectin' the engine… for repairs," said Ladderman without thinking. A quick glance by Dan caused him to study his toes intently.

"You aren't here t' fix it!" yelled Jobson. "You're here t' take the damn thing apart, and place the pieces in that scrap wagon! Don't they tell you wot yer supposed to be doin' at that office? Get them scrappers' torches an'—"

A telephone call at the watchman's shack interrupted his tirade. He strode over to the shack and was engaged in a hot conversation for several minutes (with the MSC office?). This gave Dan the opportunity he needed.

"Any more slip-ups like Ladderman's and we could end up blowing the whole scheme! Keep them totes outta sight. An' remember, Plan B." Actually, there was no 'Plan B', but it sounded good. No one asked about it either. "We can't fail now! This is our chance."

Jobson hurried over to the six silent men. "I got t' go to another yard for a time. You know wot you must do. I expect you to be well into it by the time I get back." And with that, Jobson was gone.

Dan waited a few minutes while the old Scot made his rounds, inspecting the fencing, noting what work was taking place, and which track other workers were using. The scrap metal business was doing quite well, and there was much activity in the yard. DOSE and its devious plan were but a small microcosm of Bonehead Scrappers… so when Dan thought it best, he signalled Oily Oil and Big Jake out of the main gate to a secluded site near the fence. They had placed rented sandblasting equipment behind a brick-walled warehouse, and now wheeled it into the yard.

"Come on, let's really get t' work!" encouraged Dan as the machine was started, using a petrol motor.

Meanwhile, Chalky had the excursion special well in hand and it was doing 60 mph. Back in the carriages, the members of the Second Street Railway Enthusiasts were engaged in a spirited conversation as to the merits of their respective wheel arrangements. This had all the earmarks of a previous evening. The idiot on the speaker (Prompter) tried to stop the building argument.

"I hear s-something. Now, Members, pl-please refrain fr-from this… terrible harangue…."

"Here, who's that on the speaker?" asked a Bobo in the second coach.

"Sounds like that fool from that railway we're going to," said the elder Smythe-Jones.

"Somebody should shut him up," implored another Bobo in the same carriage, a few rows down from the first complainer.

"Done!" said a Coco, sitting across the aisle from him. He got up, yanked the speaker off the wall, and hurled it out of an open gangway. It hit a guard's van of a passing goods train and bounced off the steps, falling to the ballast. "Louts," grumbled the guard.

The 'fool' taken care of, an antiphonal chorus began as it had before.

"Bobos!"

"Cocos!"

"Bobos!"

"Cocos!"

Soon the entire train was thus engaged, save the steam enthusiasts. A general melee ensued with much spirited pugilistic activity on both sides of the aisles. As the train passed through Wych Hazelton Station, some waiting passengers on the platform, noting the fight, and being ignorant of the facts, hastily reported what they had seen to the stationmaster. He telephoned BR Police, and the decision was made to halt the special at Madd Dogg. Chalky was told over the radio to stop there, but was not given a reason. However, a signal check slowed him down before he could arrive. What he did not know was that a signal failure had occurred behind him, which would influence certain events yet to happen….

Now it must be observed that Fate had a mind of its own, and today was no exception. The Special had stopped several tracks over from Bonehead Scrappers, where the DOSE members were successfully employing the sandblaster. Looking at the engine, shorn of its builder's plate, number indicators, etc. and now some paint off its left side, it was clear that the six diligent diesel enthusiasts had tried to make the most of their time.

Dan ordered the sandblaster turned off and began directing his men to apply primer to the section of 'good metal'. Cans of primer suddenly appeared from the totes, along with brushes. It was at this point that Jobson made his second appearance. At first, he didn't notice anything strange, as many workers were engaged, but when he saw the telephone lines cut, and his MSC workers applying primer to something they were supposed to be dismantling, he just couldn't believe it.

Oily Oil, looking back towards the watchman's shack, was the first to spot Jobson, who was coming at a run.

"He's back, the ruddy blighter!" called Oily Oil. Diesel Dan calmly put down his brush, aimed the sandblaster at Jobson, and hit the switch. Sand rained down at Jobson, who was forced to take cover behind the watchman's shack.

Through a mix-up of orders, Inspector Hastli and two BR Police arrived at Wych Hazelton Station "to further assess the situation". When he realized the Special had long since passed through, he knew he had to do something. Spotting an old Peak engine idling on an adjacent track, he devised a scheme whereby he would surprise the rioters.

"Come, lads, up the ladder!" he urged, startling a sleepy driver. After displaying the proper identification, the surprised engineman was ordered to follow post-haste down the track after the Special. A quick call confirmed permission to proceed, and as the engine gathered speed, the Inspector's eyes gleamed with delight. He'd board the Special at Madd Dogg, subdue the varletry, and write up his report with a flourish. Yes, he'd make sure it would come out right.

Jobson managed to scamper out of the yard and telephone the local constabulary. He was advised to remain out of harm's way, yet stay close by (!). Diesel Dan, having seen Jobson run away, turned off the sandblaster and resumed application of the primer, along with his five dedicated chums.

A siren was heard wailing in the distance. As it grew louder, the six had a sinking feeling that trouble was headed their way.

"Don't worry, I can keep them at bay for a long time," assured Dan.

The little car pulled into the yard. By this time DOSE had attracted the attention of some of the other workers in the yard, but seeing Dan and his sandblaster, and his ability to use it, they kept a wary distance. It was at this moment that Dan hit the switch again. The target was in for quite an ordeal. Sand quickly penetrated the cheap grill and flimsy plastic of the car which left gaps where there should have been none. The fan blades spewed sand all over the engine compartment. The car's computer, sensing that something was terribly wrong, shut everything down. The men inside dared not try to get out.

A distant but anxious diesel horn announced the impending arrival of the Peak engine with Inspector Hastli and his men. Deltic Dibble, having heard the horn and wandered round to the entrance of the yard, thought that the sound indicated that something was very wrong. He noted the stopped Special and began entertaining imaginary scenarios, all tragic. He stumbled out of Bonehead Scrappers and seeing no other train activity, ran to where the waiting train had been halted on the nearby track. As he glanced to his left, he observed a solitary figure farther away, waiting by a switch stand. Dibble ran as fast as his thick legs would allow until he reached the stranger, breathless and more than anxious. Dibble pointed to the train and the approaching engine wildly.

"The train! The other train! The—"

"An' who might you be?" asked the switch tender from the nearby marshalling yard.

Before Dibble could blurt out a reply, he pulled the handle, and Dibble heard the clack-clack as the metal moved into a new position.

"Got a call… signals out, extra movement. Goin' too fast. Not to worry," he said calmly.

"But the train! He'll crash!"

"Die-verted. He kin coast to a stop in there." The switch tender pointed to Bonehead Scrappers, where a few sidings were still empty. "Got permission."

Dibble ran back to Bonehead Scrappers, or tried to. He had to be extremely careful to avoid the sandblaster, still on. He did this by slipping behind the watchman's shack, the same way Jobson had managed to scamper out.

The constant blaring from the oncoming engine had the other DOSE members' attention. They froze in terror, thinking that it would strike the waiting train. By this time, Dibble had stumbled back to his friends, but was unable to speak for a few minutes. Then the driver, seeing that his speed was excessive, frantically tried to slow the engine down. Imagine their state of mind when the Peak careened off into a siding, rolled down into Bonehead Scrappers Yard, and slammed into the Deltic as they scrambled for cover! The rusting engine was thrown up against the buffers at track's end with a horrible crunch. The Peak wore a strange new design on its twisted cab and went through a serious revision of its own. Miraculously, no one on board was seriously injured as they all had jumped once the engine had entered the yard. The driver dragged himself up the ladder to shut the engine down. He then wobbled and fell to the gritty earth below.

All this threw the little band into a panic. They dropped their tools, abandoned the sandblaster, and grabbed their pilfered artefacts while running for cover behind the Special. At that moment Chalky was given permission to proceed, and the brakes were released. Oily Oil noticed an open gangway in the last carriage, and without approval from Dan, climbed aboard. The others dumbly followed, Dan being the last to clamber up the steps. Although they could not help but notice that a fight was going on, the shock of the previous few minutes was too intense for them to say or do anything.

During this interim, the 'fool', having failed to subdue anyone with his queasy pleading for peace, attempted to walk through the carriages, holding up his wet, sweaty hands as a sign for all hostilities to cease. He was promptly thrown off the train which was just now gathering speed, and ended up in a foetal position. He began walking in a dazed state of mind into Bonehead Scrappers Yard. Inspector Hastli, not knowing who he was, attended to the shutting off of the sandblaster, and his men were seeing to the occupants of the now moribund police car. Prompter wandered over to the engineman who lay crumpled in a heap; he needed medical attention. Later he walked in a zig-zag fashion to the Inspector and tugged on his coat sleeve.

"Th-that m-man needs a… doctor."

"And who are you?" the Inspector asked. "Was you on the train that just left, or is you one of those blokes who was paintin' the engine?"

Prompter had no clear explanation of who he was or what he was doing at Bonehead Scrappers, being dazed from his ejection. Hastli was rightfully suspicious, but was reluctant to arrest him for anything initially, despite Jobson's later insistence, who now emerged from safety. Finally the Inspector decided to take Prompter down to the local station for questioning. He was unable to supply anything concrete, and spent his first and only night in jail.

Upon arriving at Madd Dogg, Chalky halted the Special at Platform 2. About 20 BR Police, armed with short clubs, boarded the carriages. They took over the situation quickly, arresting approximately half of the riders. While those who were unlucky enough to be caught still fighting were escorted off the train to waiting vans, the six DOSE members quietly slipped off the gangway of the last carriage, found the nearby Madd Dogg Inn, and got terribly soused over their misfortune. After being thrown out by the surly owner, who had listened to their rantings for too long, they trudged back to the station. Fearing for their safety, they split up, taking different trains at odd hours, back to their respective homes. Oily Oil went south to Kent, Deltic Dibble headed back to Newcastle, Big Jake O'Flaherity went home to Belfast, Bob 'Brake' Cuthbert took off for Cornwall, and Dan, well, somewhere in East London called Pudding Lane, where there was a decided absence of bake shops. Having kept their addresses in a faded old notepad, Dan eventually tracked them down, but the brief history of DOSE must now be brought to a close – for now.

Chalky marvelled at the numbers of passengers being led off his train. "Go see wot the deuce they're bein' arrested for," he barked to Sedge. Of course, Sedge jumped at the order, clambered down the ladder, and asked the first policeman he saw what the whole matter was about.

"You ignoramus. Half of these blokes have been fighting tooth and nail since you chaps passed through Wych Hazelton."

"You don't say!" was Sedge's answer. After hearing what the fighting was about, he quickly returned to the cab.

When Chalky heard the news, he lit a cigar and carelessly threw his match out of the window. "See, I told you these louts were bloody crazy."

"An' you was right, you was," answered his mate. "They was fightin' over Bobos and Cocos. An' some o' them Bobbies is stayin' on the train, they is!"

"Let's hope we can get outta 'ere soon. Blue-Ped-on-Riveredge ain't too far. An' the sooner I get these nuts off me train, the better."

At the Korkerhill and Spaniel Downss, festivities were being made ready. Hired clowns were waiting to greet the younger enthusiasts from other invited clubs. Mounted hunters were paid to see that the visitors did not trespass on nearby farms. Dogs were placed in kennels at the Spaniel Downss Station to provide 'ambience'. (Cocker spaniels had been raised commercially at one time in the area's history.) The Food Hut and Souvenir Shop, tiny buildings located also at Spaniel Downss, were stocked in anticipation of good sales. Two tank engines had been fired up but left in shed. A guard's van had been coupled onto one of the engines for rides – the five o'clock surprise. Vintage, restored rolling stock had been placed at the aforenamed station, and even an actor was hired to resemble the good Count Okropoli-Simkovitch, clad in period clothes. He was supposed to make a speech about the importance of the Railway, but not before

Bookley was to give an orientation lecture.

But the Special was late because of the signal check and the unexpected delay at Madd Dogg. The ‘bus drivers at Madd Dogg Station, having wandered off in search of refreshment, had time for another round or two before Chalky brought the Special into the station 48 minutes late. It wasn’t his fault; he had no control over what had transpired in the past few hours. Sedge had failed to get another chance with the horn or driving the engine, but he figured that since he was buying Chalky’s dinner, he would get his chance… later.

The quieter half of the Second Street Railway Enthusiasts Club filed off the train and into one of the open ‘busses. They sat there for a few minutes before they realized there was no driver. An astute young man, being somewhat acquainted with the ways of the world, went off in search of the drivers. Following his instinct, and passing the now full Madd Dogg Inn, he discovered them inside the Workingman’s Friend.

When the three returned to the station, it was concluded that one ‘bus was sufficient to convey the enthusiasts to Spaniel Downss Station. The other driver, who was apparently relieved of his duty, turned round and headed back to the Workingman’s Friend for a few more rounds. Only later, when he tried to negotiate the roundabout eight miles away from the ‘bus depot, did he realize that he had had a bit too much. After squashing a parked Austin Mini and flattening numerous hazard signs, he managed to drive his ‘bus into low-lying Guss Fountain. Old Guss had been something of a character while he was alive, but never did he think half of a ‘bus would end up in a fountain named in his honour.

Driblett didn’t lose his job over this, despite loud protestations from the owner of the squashed Mini, but he was suspended without pay for 30 days.

As the one ‘Jumbo Tourbus’ made its way to the preserved railway, some of the members on board noticed that the skies were clouding up. Old Dickerson shook his head. “Be rainin’ by four o’clock this very afternoon,” he sighed. While several others chose to disagree with him, they kept their opinions to themselves in light of recent events. No one wanted anything else to go wrong….

Bobo Bic Narclay, President of this illustrious group, was about on the verge of despair. As he stared ahead at the road before him, he wondered about the ramifications of the past few hours. Members of his Club arrested for fighting on a BR train… and it had been chartered especially for them! Would that be the end of charters? He had been informed of the 'missing' speaker incident and Prompter being thrown off the train at the signal check. He thought about how these things would generate more bad publicity than he could handle. The fall-out was mind-boggling. What happened to those pledges of non-violence all members had made? He remembered that he had put the signed papers, handled at a special meeting Thursday night before the trip, in a file in his dusty house. Well, he would just have to purge the ranks, wouldn't he? Members in Good Standing versus Members in Question.

But that was a task for another day. He hoped the afternoon could be salvaged and perhaps enjoyed. He thought about the chaps on board with him and concluded he had nothing to worry about. He closed his eyes and settled back in his front seat for the remaining minutes while Dopwell piloted the quiet 'bus to its destination.

At 3:30 they pulled up to Spaniel Downss Station. A hungry crowd exited the 'bus, queued up to the ticket office, showed their Club identifications, paid their 22 pence under Bic's watchful eye, and received their souvenir tickets. Other enthusiasts and members of the general public were seen milling about, the restored carriages on the far track garnering most of their attention and photographs. But the Second Streeters were at present not allowed to gain the platform. They were held behind a wobbly fence so that Bookley could provide his lecture. He met the group by the ticket office, but found that the gate which led to the platform had somehow become jammed. Bobo Bic made an offhand excuse for the members who were 'detained'.

Bookley began his orientation lecture, much in the same tone as before, he on one side of the fence, the Second Streeters on the other.

It was at this point that the clouds decided to open up and the rain began in earnest. Greasepaint ran down costumes as clowns frantically searched for cover. When Count Okropoli-Simkovitch came over to make his speech, the rain softened the glue on his face and his beard fell off. A Second Street Railway Enthusiast knocked over part of the wobbly fence and the crowd streamed past Bookley, looking for shelter from the now pelting rain. The Station had quickly filled up with other enthusiasts and members of the general public, so they converged on the Souvenir Shop. Once everything had been bought, they became restless, and, suddenly remembering their want of provision, descended upon the tinier Food Hut.

While they ate their fill, Bookley saw his chance. Having been humiliated at the meeting Tuesday night, and almost losing his job for agreeing to the 22 pence admission price, he had sworn he'd somehow get even. Bookley sneaked over to the Food Hut, then locked the visitors inside. He could be seen through a glazed window, laughing and pointing.

The more claustrophobic members, feeling anxious, began pressing and banging against the flimsy door. Others put their backs to the wall, awaiting their release. Unbeknownst to them, the Food Hut had been constructed of less than sturdy material, and the door with its adjacent wall suddenly gave way. The men tried to move quickly out as the corrugated pink plastic roof, shorn of its supports, fell into the Hut, which caused the rest of the teetering structure to collapse.

Bookley screamed in horror as the Food Hut caved in, threw down his ice cream, and ran away behind the parked carriages. Bobos and Cocos, having spotted his leering and laughing behaviour prior to the Hut's collapse, were off in hot pursuit.

An unknown enthusiast discovered the kennels, and wanted to "pet the doggies". They were somehow released and overran the platform, causing an awful fracas. The staff made a fruitless effort to round up the pups, scattered as they were.

While all this was happening, Old Dickerson had located the shed, and led several steam men to it. "We've come t' take a look in there," he said to a wet stripling armed with a pitchfork, guarding the doors from outside.

"There is to be no one in the shed," he said firmly.

"Wot good is a visit to a railway without doing some shed bashing?" enquired Tom Jackson, putting his hands on the barred door.

"In peril of your lives, touch it not, I tell you there's nothing in the shed," said the youth, a little less firmly.

"Drivel-dravel," said Old Dickerson, shouldering him aside. The men threw open the doors and entered the darkness therein. Old Dickerson gave a shout as the stripling barred and closed the doors behind them. "Well, bless my soul, I used t' drive one like this from time t' time on the Midland!" he said with conviction.

He gave a longing glance at the tank engine and climbed onto the footplate, issuing orders. The others responded like loyal troops under a much beloved general.

The shaken youth, intent on following his instructions, resolved to keep the doors shut and, having barred them once again from the outside, leaned two large wooden planks against them. He resumed his former position with the pitchfork, intent on keeping anyone else out, while the rain continued to soak him further.

Inside the shed, Old Dickerson seemed to take on a new dimension. He felt the years roll away as he moved about the footplate with the ease and agility of someone 30 years his junior. "Right, lads, let's take her out o' the shed an' save these children the trouble! Jackson, open the doors!" But Jackson could not open the doors as they were barred. Old Dickerson checked his pocket watch; it was five o'clock, and the engine was due to be parked next to Spaniel Downss Station for rides… which he did not know.

"So, we're locked in? Not for long!" The steam men climbed aboard the guard's van as he blew one quick whistle, released the brakes, and advanced the regulator. The shed doors splintered to pieces as the tank engine smashed its way through, scattering wood left and right. The stripling flung his pitchfork down and fled the scene, thinking that the little train was going to run him over. Thoroughly surprised and shocked staff and visitors looked on in amazement as the 'Five o'clock Surprise' gathered speed quickly and breezed down the track past Spaniel Downss Station. Bookley, having been caught and pummelled by persistent Bobos and Cocos, fainted while enthusiasts stood by and cheered, thinking that the whole thing had been staged.

"By George, I feel like I'm alive again! And a fire going, too!" shouted Old Dickerson as he urged the engine to even greater speed. The men in the guard's van surveyed the retreating scene behind them and concluded that no one would be following them soon. They were only partly right. They had forgotten that another tank engine was on standby in shed (and eventual display) as part of the 'Five O'Clock Surprise'. After ten minutes of chaos, several Korkerhill and Spaniel Downss staff boarded No 2 and headed off in pursuit of the renegade engine and its crew. They could not make up the lead Old Dickerson had on them. But once he passed Korkerhill Station he knew the line would soon end. As he rounded the next bend in the track, he eased the regulator back. Sure enough, the track ended abruptly at the base of Korkerhill. A firm application of the brakes slowed the train to an easy stop.

"Right, lads, everybody out!" he called to his friends in the guard's van behind him. The men surveyed their surroundings and then scrambled up Korkerhill. Reaching the other side, they found themselves on a major highway. Old Dickerson, still in an animated state, flagged down a large red lorry with a green tarpaulin. The driver said he was going to London. Would he mind giving the gaffers a lift? They agreeably settled down under the protective tarpaulin, and while the rain continued its determined descent and the tyres of the lorry sang their high-pitched song, Old Dickerson chuckled and confessed, "I haven't had that much fun since I took 'Lizzie' out for a test run! A thoroughly enraged Korkerhill footplate staff found the abandoned engine 20 minutes later. They angrily split up, reversed both engines, and drove them slowly back to shed.

Back at Spaniel Downss, Bic Narclay was beyond any mortal help. Not only were half of his Club cooling their heels in custody, Old Dickerson had partially wrecked an engine shed, commandeered an engine and guard's van, and had driven it with glee all the way to Korkerhill. A fence had been knocked down, Count Okropoli-Simkovitch had lost his beard, 20 cocker spaniels had been lost, Bookley had been seized and assaulted, and the Food Hut had caved in. He did not know the whereabouts of the speaker belonging to Jae and Javits, or where Prompter was. Then there were the other things he didn't know about: a smashed 'Jumbo Tourbus', a driver suspended, an engineman in hospital, a Peak engine seriously damaged, a destroyed Deltic, a moribund police car, and lastly, a little railway society (temporarily) disbanded. To say "it had been quite a day" was to barely scratch the surface.

Chalky and Sedge did eventually get what was left of the Club back home. Sedge got to pilot the train into the station, but his liberal use of the horn and eagerness with the brakes limited further indulgences by Chalky.

## CHAPTER THREE
# The Deltic Disaster Revisited

It was a cool, wet, damp evening in the heart of Wales in a village with a name most Englishmen could not pronounce. The year had worn on to summer's end. Diesel Dan, having fled Pudding Lane due to several unpaid bills, including three months' rent, had also abandoned his occupation of dishwasher at Ned's, a stone's throw from his rooms. He figured no one would look for him in such (according to him) an obscure place in the Kingdom. His compatriots, having gone back to their respective lives last spring, resumed what normalcy they could as they mourned the passing of 'Old Rust and Rivets'. As Chair of DOSE, this weighed particularly heavy on his mind. He briefly recounted the painful events which had transpired back in May. He and his fellow DOSE members had seen their metal-clad dreams literally destroyed before their very eyes; had escaped from being apprehended by Jobson and the local constabulary; had abandoned a sandblaster which they had paid a large sum to rent; then boarded a chartered special train unseen; slipped off the same at Madd Dogg; had gotten very soused, yet realized there was danger in numbers; and had split up – but not before reaffirming their post addresses and telephone numbers.

Now it was a dark, moonless night in Wales at 9:15. Dan found himself on a street corner in a quiet residential section. No one was about on such an inopportune night. The row houses were, to him, strangely silent. The old slate sidewalk he stood on was deserted and empty of all other forms of existence.

Dan suddenly remembered he hadn't eaten since that morning, before he made his getaway on a BR train, picking this village seemingly because he became restless as station after station rolled by. He shuffled down several blocks before the swaying sign of the Green Dragon beckoned him towards the end of the next street. A pint would not only taste good, but perhaps take away his keen sense of hunger.

The pub looked like something out of a 17th century painting. Its stout oaken beams and leaded glass windows lent a welcome air of stability and timelessness. It was simply too much to resist after the day and past events, including dodging the landlord and spirits shoppe owner, who had mistakenly given him credit. Dan ambled inside, observed what most of the patrons were having, and did the same. He sat wearily at the bar and took a long sip. The bartender, noting the filthy condition of his clothes, enquired about him in a roundabout fashion.

"Don't remember seeing you in 'ere before."

"I never seed you before neither," was his sullen reply. The bartender was silent. Dan panicked. Anonymity he was very anxious to preserve, and he was, for a moment, at a loss. He hadn't planned anything beyond running away from Pudding Lane to somewhere in Wales because he thought the authorities would be less likely to look for him there. But beyond that, he had thought of little else.

The bartender, not willing to be put off so easily, tried another tack. "Say, wot line o' work are you in?"

Dan knew little of Wales except for the things he had heard other people say and the usual things one correctly or otherwise associates with the region: coal mines, proud, independent people who are dark-featured, and good singers. That was all he thought he knew. So he said, "Mining." With this remark, the bar fell silent. The bartender, a large, bulky man with piercing black eyes and a thick moustache, raised one eyebrow.

"Minin', izzit?" He wiped the bar with a deliberate look of suspicion. Apparently this remark had aroused the curiosity of several patrons. One of them, a stout man in his forties, grabbed his glass, made his way to the bar, and eyed Dan with more than passing interest. Dan nervously drank his ale. He did not welcome this kind of attention. He had hoped his dirty clothes would help convince people that 'mining' was his occupation.

"So, yer a miner? Wot be the name of the firm?" Silence. "Wot's the colliery then?"

Dan's knowledge of Welsh was limited to a very small number of tune names he had seen in the hymnal at church when a youngster, and it had been some time since he had gone to a service. He searched his mind for one; then he looked at the stout man and said, "Aberystwyth."

The bartender stopped wiping down the black bar, threw the rag into a small sink, and leaned within an inch of Dan's ashen face.

"Aberystwyth!" exclaimed the stout man. "And wot be yer name?" Dan had to think fast. He pretended to flip through the hymnal again, and said, "Hyfrydol." By this time, everyone had surrounded him.

"Wot be your mother's name, then?" asked an unseen man behind him. The only other Welsh name he could remember was Llandudno, which he tried to say, but failed miserably. Roars of laughter filled the Green Dragon. The bartender clapped his hands together as Dan sank lower and lower into his seat.

"Welsh, are you? You're no more Welsh than the Irish Sea!" shouted the stout man in anger. The true Welshmen in the pub (and that was everyone to a man except Dan) unceremoniously escorted him right out the door and into the wet street. With shouts of "Miner!" and "Welshman!" the true men of Wales assailed him, until, figuring he had received enough, they decided to return to their tables.

Dan had been marked for life. Never again would he be able to go to the Green Dragon without incurring the wrath of the watchful sentinels of the land. With only a little pocket change and some dirty pound notes he had found blowing in the street, Dan had little recourse but to seat himself on the still-wet sidewalk several blocks from the Green Dragon. However, even this attempt at repose was thwarted by a dedicated constable who shooed him away, wherever that was.

The night was getting cooler. Dan had not brought a change of clothes, and the air was beginning to have its effect. He began walking until he saw steam coming from a vent in the old grey slate sidewalk.

Nearby in the street he spotted a manhole cover. A diligent search turned up a long piece of iron in an alley behind several large dust-bins. With this, he pried open the manhole, replaced the iron piece where he had found it, and crept into the hole in the street. There was no light, but his hands found a large steam pipe and slowly, painfully, he discovered a ledge which he could crawl onto. The warmth from the steam pipe was sufficient enough for him to keep warm in his slouched position. Thus he spent the night in warm dejection.

The next morning, Dan was awakened by a loud jarring sound somewhere above him. Unbeknownst to him, a lorry driver with a cautious way about him had noted the 'misplaced' manhole cover, parked his lorry, and had pushed it back in place with the handle of a shovel he kept in the back of his conveyance. It took Dan several minutes to ascertain this, but he slowly began to realize he knew of no other way out. Well, being trapped under the street in a Welsh village was definitely *not* part of the plan. Now what was he to do?

Dan panicked momentarily and felt sick to his stomach. His faculties began to work again after a lorry was heard starting up and pulling away. The only thing he could think of was to follow the passageway. But which way should he go? He selected the way ahead, and not long afterwards (in complete darkness) he felt the big steam pipe take an abrupt turn to the right, to go in (or out) of some building. He then slowly, painfully, pushed himself on cautiously for what seemed like hours, keeping his hands in front of him for protection. But eventually he reached the stage where success of some kind was needed for the possibility of hope to remain alive, and as he had not yet tasted the fruit of triumph, he simply gave up, leaned against the solid and sturdy brick wall, and cried out in complete despair.

A dull thud somewhere nearby caused him to look up quickly in reaction, but for that instant he had forgotten that he could not see anything at all. Feeling his way towards the direction of the source of the sound, he found a space in the brick wall which gave way to a set of ancient iron doors with a tiny hole in each. Even these small amounts of light caused his eyes to blink several times.

With more than an urgent sense of desperation, he yanked on the door to his right. It was tightly closed, and with years of rust, it would not move. The other one barely budged, but it was enough for him to eventually push forward so that he could squeeze through. The doors were actually once an entrance for workmen when the underground water system was built, but after it was completed, the passageway had never been sealed.

And where had that life-saving sound come from? Dan found himself walking up some barely discernible brick steps covered with long grasses. His eyes hurt with the light so much he had to shield the morning sun with his hand. Once his eyes could stand the light, he looked around the immediate area. The buildings and their auras spoke of an earlier time of prosperity and activity. The noise which had roused him from despair came from a feed and corn mill where a lorry had pulled up for the receiving of goods. Two brothers were loading dairy feed in burlap bags onto the weathered floorboards of their Leyland. What could he say to them in the way of thanks? Would they laugh in derision, or would they understand?

He began walking towards them, unsure of what he should or could say. HenWas and Brynn Trewent saw the slipshod, rough-clad individual and stopped for a moment. They looked at one another with an understanding borne of many years of close association, family ties, and hard work. Quickly they sized him up as men who are only too well acquainted with the harsh realities of life can do. You reckon he'll ask us for money, was the unspoken message these two brothers shared.

"If you hadn't been bangin' round wid them feed sacks I'd be closed in there still." Dan pointed towards the ancient iron doors and brick steps he had recently emerged from.

HenWas raised an eyebrow.

"Yer own cromlech," said Brynn sharply.

"An' wot were you doin' in there anyway?" asked HenWas with more than his usual curiosity.

"I got trapped i' the tunnel and could find no way out. Some bloke put me manhole cover on so I couldn't get out." It was at this awkward juncture that he introduced himself as Dan Settles.

"That 'bloke' was me, you chunkhead," commented Brynn quickly. "We were doin' our week's errands this morning and I saw this cover sticking up. 'HenWas,' says I, 'a man could get into a terrible crack up if he were to hit that thing with a wheel.' So I stopped and put it back."

"You still didn't tell us what you were doing in there." HenWas wanted the facts and he hadn't received any kind of explanation up to this point. Dan did not dare tell him why he was in town, but he did mention that he was (nearly) penniless, out of work, and had no place to stay. So he said, "Spent the night inna fouulll place."

HenWas and Brynn winked at each other in an 'I told you so' manner.

"Well, Dan, (if that is your real name), the farm needs a spare man to help round the place. We can't offer you much except a place to sleep, hard work, and a few quid."

Dan had little choice but to agree. The brothers finished their loading and instructed Dan to find a spot in back to ride. Dan boosted himself onto the lorry, found a reasonably comfortable area between several feed bags, and lay down. Soon the rattling and swaying of the lorry over the cobbled streets lulled him to sleep. Thus the sturdy yeomen brothers found him once they parked their lorry in the old shed an hour later.

They gave him the next day off, it being the Sabbath. Dan took the time to eat, take a long bath, rest, and put on some proffered old clothes. But on Monday the brothers had him up at five, learning about all the chores that he would soon be aiding his efforts to. While Ladderman had spoken of his various duties on the Jersey farm, Dan had paid little attention to the details. HenWas decided Dan should start in the barn, and he soon found out that these chores included the milking, the feeding, the mucking out, and the hundred other tasks a dairy farmer occupies himself with. Dan's first official chore, however, was to unload the recently purchased feed into the huge, wooden bins in the barn. The burlap bags would be saved and returned to the mill the following Saturday, as was the custom. Dan stacked them next to a bin on the floor.

Once he was settled, which took a few weeks, he began writing his DOSE chaps in earnest. He felt that he had to keep the Club alive, even if it were one of scattered remains. Strangely, he could not understand why they were so reluctant to reply. Ladderman was, like himself, working on his family's dairy farm in Jersey; Dempsey 'Deltic' Dibble and family owned and operated Dibble's Bake Shop in Newcastle, where his 'Deltic Delights', cookies shaped like the very engines the Club worshipped, and topped with burnt sugar, were a local favourite. Big Jake O'Flaherity was helping his brother run a pub in Belfast; Bob 'Brake' Cuthbert was employed in a metals factory in Cornwall; and Don 'Oily Oil' Wilson drove (what else?) a petrol lorry for BP in Kent.

While plans to get together and pursue their common interests were naturally on everyone's mind, they had to put them on hold for the time being. Dan, who was known to have an occasional burst of inspiration, contacted a sympathetic member of the Second Street Railway Enthusiasts Club for information on any of the active Deltics. Nothing at present was forthcoming, but Dan was promised future postings should anything turn up. So the members of the less than merry group known as DOSE worked and waited for weeks.

One bright day, when Dan was mucking out some stalls, a letter with a London postmark arrived at the farm. If only Dan had known what its contents were! There would be absolutely no delay in the ritual of receiving, reading, marking, and inwardly digesting what was within.

The sympathetic member of the London Club had some unbelievable news. The younger Smythe-Jones had done some investigating on his own, and what he had written caused Dan to leap out of his chair. It was reported that the scraps and pieces of the old Deltic were still at Bonehead Scrappers. The scrap metal had been bought by another firm, and the wagon was to be towed there within 20 days.

Would Dan be interested in making the trip to London to view the remains while it was still possible?

Well, it was all he could do to contain himself. Frantically and without a solid explanation, he borrowed the lorry, heading straight for a small concern, where he nervously sent off five hastily written telegrams.

The following week was filled with a flurry of activity and chores which were rushed through to completion. Dan's antics, coupled with the letters which made their way to the farm, gave rise to brotherly speculation. So on Friday night, once the dishes had been washed by Dan, dried, and put away, he was called to council in the parlour. Brynn had lit a fire to take the chill off the room, as it was now early Fall. HenWas had lit his pipe and was in his favourite hand-carved, wooden chair where his father and grandfather before him had reposed after a long day's labours. Brynn assumed an unusual position by the fire which one would normally describe as cramped, but suited him well.

"So, Dan, what's all this, the letters coming in from all over the Kingdom?" queried HenWas calmly, yet there was no question of the seriousness in his voice.

Dan once again became flustered. The last time he had lied in this Welsh county, he had met with an unceremonious exit from the Green Dragon. No longer could he walk that street with any sense of ease. A split second of indecision lingered to half a minute; then he realized lying to these honest, hardworking men would be a sin. So he broke his silence, and told them everything, from the beginning of the Club through its past debacles, which included the disaster at Bonehead Scrappers and the scattering of its members, done clandestinely.

HenWas gazed into the fire with a twinkle in his eyes; Brynn eased himself into a chair next to his brother and remarked, "An outlandish tale… if it be true." Dan wildly assured him it was. Then he begged the brothers for one week off before the situation at Bonehead Scrappers changed. After this plea, HenWas and Brynn eyed each other the same way they had for years. HenWas put his pipe down and slowly turned to Dan. "You have been a good worker, Dan. We took you in and you do a day's work without complaint. The dishes shine like mirrors once we give 'em to you. Never did see our kitchen look so good."

"Dishwashin' and such been my occupation," inserted Dan. "Can cook a bit as well."

HenWas continued. "We all want a day or two off on occasion. But t' ask now when you've got all your chores—"

"Ah, let the man go," said Brynn as he waved Dan off. "We managed without him before. We can manage without him now. He's a fool t' be running after a torn up engine that won't turn a wheel again."

HenWas filled his pipe with that brown mixture he and his forebears enjoyed. After a slight pause, his dark grey eyes seemed to say it all.

"Well, Dan, we are of one mind. I don't think you're meaning t' be ungrateful to us, but that's how it's coming out. So – go if you must – but don't show up at our door if you're not back in a week's time."

Dan gratefully acknowledged the grudging assent of his employers and put his tentative plans into motion. By a week's time, he and his fellow Club members were ready to make their collective move. He did take Oily Oil's suggestion of meeting once again at the Madd Dogg Inn, site of their earlier demise. At first Deltic Dibble objected to this as an unnecessary expense, but Dan successfully persuaded him to agree. Once again, suddenly sick or dead relatives materialized before startled employers, as well as the begged week's leave "to settle the matters in want".

One morning in late September, the six DOSE members left their still dark domiciles (Ladderman and Big Jake had left earlier than the others), bought their tickets to Madd Dogg, dreamed about food, cursed their fate, or wondered what might have been if the object of their affection had not met with such a tragic and violent end. Dan had warned them to be circumspect in their speech and manner, and so the stationmaster at Madd Dogg thought it rather odd that off every other train between eleven and four, there alighted a bloke with an upturned collar and a cap pulled low over the face. However, he was too busy with routine matters to devote any real time for rumination.

Once the suspicious-looking characters moved one by one off the platform, they quietly repaired to the Madd Dogg Inn where Dan had decided to hold court in a little-used back room. The last one to arrive was, strangely enough, not Big Jake, but Oily Oil. He had missed his earlier connecting train in London.

Over mugs of ale and modest portions of fish and chips, Dan officially convened the meeting of the once nearly defunct club known as DOSE amid several rounds of “Cheers!” and calls for more of the same. After the conviviality and the familiar sense of belonging were experienced to a satisfactory level by the little group, Dan genially reiterated the details of what their good friend, the younger Smythe-Jones, had passed along. Dissensions ensued as to how best to obtain access to Bonehead Scrappers. While the ‘MSC Scheme’ had worked well before (it *had* gained them access), Bob ‘Brake’ Cuthbert strongly objected to and advised against using this avenue again. The group suddenly became silent, as no one had thought this far along. After too much ale and not enough food, Deltic Dibble held up one of his chubby, pasty, white hands.

“Here, that bloke who was on the watch was a Scot, weren’t he? Well, I say we go in there like we’re tryin’ t’ find our long-lost relative.”

“And how d’ you propose we go about bein’ like we’re Scots?” thundered Big Jake.

Dibble held up his other chubby paw. “Jus’ a little stroll t’ the second hand shops in town’ll give us the kilts an’ stockings.”

“Ah, man, you’re out of your bloomin’ mind,” jeered Ladderman. “And what if we did find ’em? Who here is going to say they’d wear one? Janmais.”

“I seed a shop down the road a ways which advertises ’em, as if anyone round ’ere would actually buy ’em,” noted Oily Oil.

“Well, it just so ’appen this town is full o’ Scots for some reason,” said Dan as carefully as possible.

“I wonder if the distillery’s t’ blame,” laughed Bob. “You know how they love that whiskey.”

"Not all Scots drink whiskey," cautioned Oily Oil.

Dibble stood up, placing his pasty hands on the beaten and worn table. "Well, let's 'ear a better plan from ye."

Silence.

"Then let us buy the kilts and look sharp." Dibble sat down heavily. Ladderman objected but was outvoted. The new plan was dubbed 'The Scotch Kilt Scheme'.

Dan staggered to open the door on iron hinges which swung to everyone's right. The motley crowd tottered to the shop in question, where an utterly surprised clerk sold them six different sets of kilts and stockings in six different tartans. They slept off their endeavour back at the Madd Dogg Inn, too inebriated to cause any noise beyond their collective snores. The following morning found them departing for London a few hours later than they had planned.

On the way, they changed into their authentic Scots garb in the loo, one at a time, foolishly discarding their pants, which were later found by staff. The rest of the journey was spent practising what they thought was "how Scots talked". Curious stares from other passengers did nothing to dissuade them from their nearly hilarious attempts at the brogue. A vignette of their conversations would have revealed something like this:

"Well, they say 'Aye' a lot."

"Yes, that's right. Aye. Aye. Aye Aye!"

"No, Ladderman, they don't say 'Aye Aye'. That's sailor's talk."

"Right. I should know that, one of my brothers was in Her Majesty's Navy."

"Wot else do they say?"

"They're always recitin' some poet of theirs… Bruns, Browns, Bowers… somebody like that."

"Let's ask somebody in London 'bout that!"

"They're all Presbyterians or Catholics."

"But wot else do they say?" There was a pause while they tried to come up with more examples….

"Aye. Aye Aye!"

"Nooo, not 'Aye Aye!' 'Aye' by itself!"

"They say whiskey."

"Whis-kee. WHIS-kee."

"Wot's the capital o' Scotland?"

"It's not no foreign place."

"No, whis-KEE!"

"Aye. Oim's frum Scootlund."

"Mee, too… frum Inverr... niss."

"Well, I be frum Eedinburoo."

"Wait. If we say we're from Scotland when we visit this old codger, then we better agree on wot city we're from."

"How can we decide what city we're from if we don't know where he is from?"

"Aye. Oim's frum Scootlund."

"Noo, it's Scootlund."

"Aye. Aye Aye!"

"Shut up, Ladderman!"

"Oy, pass me some Scootch, mahn!"

"D'ya drink it wid waterrr?"

It went on its almost pitiful way until the train rattled its way into Euston. There they departed, stopping momentarily as Dan sailed into a shop and purchased a book of unknown authorship. They caught the backward glance of a BR policeman who made a mental note of some "odd-looking Scots". They transferred to an old m.u. which took them to Factory Furnace Station. After nearly pushing themselves out of the old single compartment-style carriage, they rushed off towards their Mecca, only to discover it was eight o'clock, and the old Scot, if he still worked there, had wended his way home several hours before their very conspicuous arrival. Deciding that they had come this far and that there was no turning back, they spent an uncomfortable vigil with their backs to the yard, courtesy of the nearby brick-walled warehouse, the very one where the sandblasting equipment had been hidden, but, strangely enough, "was not there".

Dawn broke the darkness but could only manage a grey reception for the awakening world. O'Flaherity took it as a sign, but the others dismissed the notion as ridiculous. After all, hadn't they gotten together at Madd Dogg "despite the odds", formulated a plan to get past the old Scot, and weren't they literally at the very gates themselves?

When all the Deltic admirers rose stiffly at 7:00, Oily Oil posed a sobering question… "We didn't bring tools, not a spanner between us. What'll we do once we get in there?"

"Wot do we need spanners for? The engine is all bits and pieces," objected Ladderman. He was kicked for his sobriety.

"We'll use the ones in the shed," Dibble said emphatically.

"How the Deuce d' you know there are any in there?" roared Big Jake, who suddenly had come to life again.

"I seed 'em in there last time we was 'ere!" shouted Dibble.

"That were spring. Wot makes you think that they're still in there?" asked Bob Brake.

"An' where are we gonna put them parts *this* time? We forgot t' bring our totes," noted Oily Oil.

"How are we going to put all the engine pieces in totes!" yelled Ladderman.

"I say let's not argue about it all now," said Dan. "Keep yer voices down! There's the little matter of our Scotch accents t' practise."

The little band of would-be 'Highlanders' prated on with some attempts at success, but largely confined themselves to visages of yesterday's moribund conversations held on the up train to London. While they were engrossed, they failed to notice the long-hoped-for old watchman, who quietly unlocked the battered steel mesh gates to the road and then to the permanent way. After peering warily into the yard as if he suspected someone was in its environs, and despite a strong hunch that would not leave him, the old Scot (MacLeish was his surname) settled into his familiar routine, albeit a little uneasy. He looked at the daily sheet of work scheduled and noted that the BR local would be by for the scrap wagon on the far track, going to Inchey's. The other wagons were not yet filled with the various remains of other wrecked conveyances.

Oily Oil happened to look up and spotted the open gates, which invited their illegal yet eager entrance. Reassuring themselves that they had their story straight, a nervous yet determined group of Deltic admirers passed through the road gate and approached the watchman's shack. What they were going to do once they got into the yard had yet to enter their cloudy minds. Their drive to arrive failed to provide them with any concrete plan to 'Remove and restore our Deltic'. How to convince MacLeish to voluntarily give up the remains had not occurred to them; not one single strategy had made its way into 'The Scotch Kilt Scheme'. Still they pressed forward. Vague notions seemingly blotted out the deplorable condition of the engine and precluded any sobering thoughts beyond hazy abstractions.

Ladderman, a little ahead of the others, reached the shack first, knocked on the weathered door, and cried, "Ahoy!"

"You blockhead. That's sailor's talk!" shouted Oily Oil, who was feeling a little volatile.

The door creaked open and the true Scot peered out at the Pretenders. "Go on wi' ye now, yer on private property an'—" He was about to wave them off until he caught sight of the Scottish garb, awkwardly worn. "Well, bless my soul, and in London, too. Scots!" The old man almost jumped out of the door. "Where ye hail from? Wot'er ye doin' in these parts?"

"Inverrniss!"

"And Eedinburoo!"

Not only had they forgotten their agreed on origin, Ladderman forgot to say his 'Aye' just once.

"Yer a strange one, mahn. Never did 'ear a Scot say 'Aye Aye' unless he served in Her Majesty's Navy."

No one capitalized on this as an out.

Dibble blurted out next in a wavering accent, "We keim awl thee wayee ta foind air uncle. It's yoo, ahfter awl these yearzz!"

MacLeish stopped smiling. He began to eye the restless band with a keen air of suspicion. "Lissen 'ere. I got no nephews, and look at you." He paused. "That's MacGregor, Dress Stewart, Lindsay, Black Watch, MacCullen, and Royal Stewart. I got no nephews, I'm not from Inverness or Edinburgh, and nobody in my family wears any o' them tartans!"

O'Flaherity said quietly, "Maybe he's Catholic." Ok, thought Dan, here goes.

"Say, Nuncle, wot's a Presbyterian?'

MacLeish faced Dan sternly. "I know what one is."

That should have been fair warning. Instead, Dan failed to heed the sign.

"Half Scotch and half ginger ale."

The old Scot picked up a shovel and swung it at Dan, clipping him on the leg and causing him to fall. "I'll thank 'e not to insult my religion."

O'Flaherity sagely advised, "He's not Catholic."

Dan, still in a lengthened state on the ground, spoke next.

"How d'ya know when yer round a bunch of Methodists?"

Dead silence.

"Where there are four, there's always a fifth."

The old Scot threw away his shovel in a fit of laughter. He staggered back to his shack and leaned against the door sill, gasping for breath.

Dan, sensing an opportunity, pulled a small volume of Burns' poetry from his coat pocket, hastily purchased at Euston after an even more hasty enquiry as to "what Scotch people like t' read an' quote". He quickly turned to a page and read out loud:

*"Let other Poets raise a fracas*
*'Bout vines an' wines an' drunken Bacchus,*
*An' crabbit names an' stories wrack us,*
*An' grate our lug;*
*I sing the juice Scots bear can mak us,*
*In glass or jug."*

MacLeish stopped laughing. He no longer heard a halfwit trying the brogue. He got a misty look in his eyes, for all he heard was the soul of Scotland.

"Bobby Burns, as I live and breathe," he mused. "Ah, say it over for me."

But Diesel Dan had lost his place and found another poem. He began:

*"When Death's dark stream I ferry o'er,* (MacLeish joined him on the second line)
*A time that surely shall come;*
*In Heaven itself I'll ask no more,*
*Than just a Highland welcome."*

MacLeish stared off with an unusual look, one born of a longing for something or someone far away. Dan found something different this time as he flipped some pages:

*"O ken ye what Meg o' the Hill has gotten?*
*An' ken ye what Meg o' the Hill has gotten?*
*She gotten a coof wi'a claut o' siller,*
*And broken the heart of the barley Miller.*
*The Miller was strappin', the Miller was ruddy;*
*A heart like a lord, and a hue like a lady;*
*The laird was a widdiefu', bleerit knurl;*
*She's left the guid fellow and taen the churl."*

"Och, mahn, a bit o' Burns amidst the heathen," murmured MacLeish. He stared off towards the edge of the yard where the connection to BR metals was visible. All eyes followed his, and their gaze took in the scene, then shifted from their former escape route to the siding where the old Peak engine had done its unintentional dirty work. While it had been pulled out and repaired, little remained of 'Old Rust and Rivets'. Some shards and bits were left under the rising weeds, and at least one bogie, though seen, was horribly twisted. Most of what was worth salvaging had already been placed in a nearby wagon belonging to Inchey's Scrap Yard, a similar concern located a few miles from their present location.

The entire situation devastated the kilt-clad brethren, and almost to a man, they turned their collective anger, disgust, and frustration towards the hapless MacLeish, who was still wafting ever upwards on the rosy clouds of the Scottish bard.

Bob Brake, spotting a coiled rope in the opened hut, deftly eased himself inside behind MacLeish, and before he realized it, had the watchman bound. It took Dibble and Oily Oil to drag him inside. This time, however, nobody bothered to disconnect the telephone wires, something which the little band would apprehend all too late.

Diesel Dan huddled his faithful, once Big Jake slammed the hut door shut with an air of finality. It was decided that an inspection of what was left of the hulk was in order, and they proceeded to the sombre site. Dibble policed the area ahead of the buffers where the track ended. "There be nothing here," he called.

"Then let's grab everything we can," yelled Bob Brake, referring to the bits before him.

"Put everything in that wagon," advised Oily Oil, pointing to Inchey's wagon. "It'll be there for safe keeping."

"There's nothing left of it except scrap," complained Ladderman. "How can we ever put it back together again?"

"Shut up, Jacob John," exclaimed Dan, irritated at this temperate statement. "Start pickin' everything up like yer told."

While the group was thusly engaged, a standard BR diesel shunter was making its cautious way through the busy yard. The engineman's mate leaped off, threw a manual switch, and clambered back on as his mate guided the engine through the points onto a rusting track.

"Don't look like the watch is even 'ere at awl," observed the driver, glancing round.

"I don't see him," answered his mate.

"Hello, looks like there's somebody over there pickin' up scraps an' such," said Chalky, back to his normal bookings since spring.

"Well, that's odd. Look at 'em! They're all wearin' kilts!" noted Sedge. Little did he know that, like MacLeish, he and Chalky had stumbled on to the group's 'Scotch Kilt Scheme'.

"I never seen the like," laughed Chalky, easing back on the regulator a bit. "They've imported a bunch of Scotchmen to pick up the trash."

Chalky and Sedge chuckled as they watched Diesel Dan & Co scurrying as quickly as they could to dump all the bits and pieces of the Deltic still on the ground in the wagon. A sharp blast from Chalky's shunter horn stopped them dead in their tracks. They hadn't anticipated anything like this happening.

"What'll we do now?" whined Deltic Dibble. "That might be the coppers like the last time we was here."

Chalky gently coasted the remaining yards to within a few steps of the scrap laden wagon.

"Here, you Scots! Where's the old man?" yelled Sedge from the cab.

Oily Oil tried to get rid of him first. "Oh, he kinder went off." His wavering brogue caused Chalky some suspicion.

"'Went off.' Don't sound like Scotch talk t' me," he quipped.

Deltic Dibble went next. "Wee keim all these wayee from Invberrborough t' see him. He's our lohng lost cousin, he izz."

"'Inverborough'? Sounds more like a Newcastle accent," observed Sedge. "Look, they're all wearing different coloured kilts. Why d' you suppose that is, Chalky?"

"These gents 'ave a funny air about 'em," Chalky said to Sedge. "Ask them again where the old man is."

"Where's the old man, the watchman? He got papers on the wagon."

Chalky leaned out the window on Sedge's side, getting a little impatient. "We're taken this wagon t' Inchey's Scrap Yard down way. Get the watchman now."

Ladderman's apparent lack of common sense allowed him to

make the following remark, wholly forgetting his 'Scotch' accent: "You can't see him. He's in the hut."

The Deltic band immediately squelched Ladderman from further illumination by pummelling him into the ground.

"Hmm. Wot we got 'ere izz... they claim t' be Scotch, they talk like Englishmen, they say they're from some strange-soundin' towns, and they mistreat their 'brother'. They're about as Scotch as me. Get over t' that hut, Sedge."

But Dan and friends had other ideas. They had waited too long for this opportunity to live past glory. Despite the overwhelming evidence to the contrary, and Ladderman's complaint which urged a doleful conclusion, the rest still clung to the notion that one day these rusting remains would (somehow) transform themselves into an engine once again.

"You can't take the wagon. We're back to reclaim wot was ours. And we're keepin' it!" yelled Bob Brake, lapsing into his own speech.

"Wot they want with that pile of junk metal in the wagon?" wondered Sedge.

"Louts. Get going, Sedge!"

The DOSE members formed a line to try to stop Sedge, but the wily engineman had a plan of his own. Chalky pelted them with pieces of ballast he kept in some old coal scuttles expressly for such a purpose. This had the effect of scattering the wavering line in an unsteady stream away from the wagon. Chalky then appeared on the engine. His expert aim allowed Sedge to make a dash for the hut. Ballast was raining down so hard that the hapless crowd had to bolt for the safety of the gate and beyond to the shelter of the same brick-walled warehouse which had afforded them modest comfort experienced the previous night and last spring.

By this time, Sedge had made his way to the grey watchman's hut, untied MacLeish, found the paperwork on Inchey's scrap wagon, telephoned the local constabulary, and headed back to the shunter.

"Damn it! We'll be 'ard pressed t' get this wagon over t' Inchey's by four with this delay and our other stops," muttered Chalky as

Sedge made the connections. "These louts'll do anything t' keep a bit o' the past. Puts me in mind o' the excurrzshun we 'ad t' rescue an' that other time we went t' Blue-Ped-on-Riveredge. Don't miss them excurrzshuns. But even 'ere, we run into these nuts. They're awl purely insane."

Sedge reflected on this candid observation quietly as Chalky eased the shunter and its consist slowly out of Bonehead Scrappers. After throwing a manual switch, passing through the points, and resetting it, the dedicated BR crew made its local pick-ups and finally delivered the solitary wagon to Inchey's at 4:08 pm. Chalky noted the time and headed back to shed, cursing "those Scotch louts" who nearly caused him to miss high tea.

Once Chalky and Sedge had departed the immediate environs and it was deemed safe to emerge from behind the safety of the brick-walled warehouse, Dan did a quick assessment of the present situation. His thoughts were suddenly interrupted by the arrival of the local constabulary (numbering three) which sent DOSE fleeing towards Factory Furnace Station, where curious passengers eyed the respective clans with either wonder or disdain. Dibble found a telephone booth and enquired about the address of Inchey's. A frantic conversation with the ticket clerk revealed a way to get within walking distance of the scrap yard. Tickets were hastily purchased.

As the m.u. pulled into the station, the police were enquiring after the motley crew. The clerk informed them of their next move. He had not been fooled by their nearly lifeless Scots accents, nor their claim to find "the best way back to Inverborough, by way of Inchey's".

After making a weary trek from Warehouse Way Station, the 'Scots' collapsed in the shadows of yet another brick-walled warehouse, not far from Inchey's, whose gates were now locked. With no food and only a few stolen sips of water at Factory Furnace Station, the situation was nearly desperate. No longer was there any hope of getting what was left of the engine and putting it back together. There was even less of a chance that they would ever get to see what was now in a secured place. Fruitless discussions on what they 'should do next' led to nothing but more frustration and anger. Some windows had stones hurled at them, an office was broken into and ransacked for food, with Ladderman refusing to take part. Curses and shouts were raised to such an extent that Dan eventually had to bring closure to the confusion which pervaded not only the warehouse they had skulked into, but the minds of those who were engaged in wanton acts. Despite entertaining some rival suggestions, including "spending the night in the scrap wagon, if the same be found in the yard", Dan told the despondent group that the Deltic was a lost cause. Wails of despair were drowned out by a noisy summons from an unknown party to "Open this barred door, or face the consequences." Dan whispered a quick plan of action: get out the back door, located by Big Jake; scatter one by one, and find their way the best they could to Warehouse Way Station. He strictly charged them not to follow one another, but use individual means to arrive at their rendezvous. Having done something like this before, the details were universally understood.

Though unfamiliar with the neighbourhood, DOSE managed to find six unrelated venues of disappearance. Thus the constabulary were frustrated in their attempts to locate and detain six plaid-clad 'Scots' whose main mission in life had been to salvage the carcass of a less than shining example of early dieseldom, and which should have died a quieter and less violent death.

Two hours later, the last kilted straggler had made his way to the faded Victorian-style brick station. An unofficial meeting, due to its haste, was convened, but came to no avail. Dan sagely advised them to give up their quest and once again return to their respective homes and lives. They filed out of the smoke-filled waiting room to Platform 2.

An old Peak engine that looked suspiciously familiar was standing on Track 2, wheezing away while the driver had gone to speak to the stationmaster about nothing important. Big Jake, who had a head for figures, finally recognized the number on the side, and remembered the diesel as the very one which had unexpectedly wreaked so much harm to their idol of worship.

Once he informed everyone that *this* was the engine that had turned their dreams into dust, a spontaneous, yet shared outbreak of sheer hate became manifested upon the hapless machine. Nearly every conceivable verbal abuse known to man was used against it, and every readily available object was hurled against it to further their objective.

After a mutual act of relief which was directed all over the left side, Ladderman quickly ascended the cab and began blowing the horn with abandon. As a few dazed people looked on in continued disbelief at the unfolding drama, all of DOSE were soon in the cab and had shut the door. Diesel Dan, having studied several engine drivers' manuals too well, released the engine brake. Then he advanced the regulator a little too fast. With a shudder and wheels momentarily slipping, the ageing loco barked black smoke from its filthy stack and slowly began moving away from the platform. Dan advanced the regulator a little more and elbowed Ladderman as he had not eased up on the horn.

"Let's give this thing the treatment it gave our own," suggested Dibble.

"We swear to wreck this thing," intoned Bob with deadly intent.

Dan, with no plan of his own and no one to guide him, went along with this new manoeuvre, dubbed 'Wreck the Peak Scheme', which was adopted without hesitation by all. But how would they accomplish this without bringing serious injury to themselves? He pondered this briefly as the miles clicked by.

Meanwhile, back at Warehouse Way Station, the driver reappeared on Platform 2 and gave everyone within earshot a taste of his extensive knowledge of the unseemly side of his vocabulary for about 5 minutes. Hurling accusations on innocent travellers and throwing dustbins at them, his vitriolic nature led him to kick the station wall in futility. Some good soul, having escaped the flying dustbins, had perforce summoned the stationmaster, who was surprised to discover Toby sans engine. Finding him inconsolable, he stalked off the platform and rang HQ with what little he could get out of the apoplectic driver.

Fifteen miles down the permanent way, in a small marshalling yard, Inspector Hastli, dimly aware that he had once somewhere run into these thieves before, prepared himself and his men along the track of the distant but approaching engine. Since his disaster with, unbeknownst to him, the very same engine last spring, his superiors had decided to keep him on a tight leash, and therefore had issued grim reminders *not* to commandeer an idling engine and give pursuit. He had issued his own orders, and this time, his well-thought-out plans garnered respect from those under him. To his credit, he had ordered a switch tender to carefully place himself in position a quarter mile farther down the track just in case. Should the errant engine run the checkpoint, he was prepared to throw a switch to divert onto a secondary yard track which came to an abrupt end.

Ten minutes went by before Ladderman's fixation with the horn was evident to anyone nearby. A flickering light pointed to the exact location of the speeding loco, and Dan, realizing that someone was nearby or on the track ahead of him, pulled back on the regulator and began applying the brake, despite howls of protest to the contrary. Hastli, seeing the engine slowing, breathed a palpable sigh of relief. He and his men planned to form a circle round the engine, once it was stopped. A passing goods driver saw the Peak and noticed the curious state the paint job was in on its left side.

"Now what?" wailed Deltic Dibble. "They've got us. Why the devil did ye stop?"

Dan had to think fast. "Let ME do the talking. Ladderman, gi' way from the horn!" He brought the engine to a stop.

Ladderman gave six long blasts and quit. He tried to sit against the driver's control stand but Dan pushed him off. Ladderman fell to the floor, but one of his legs caught Dan's left one and this pulled him down as well. As Ladderman fell, one of his gnarled hands inadvertently struck the brake lever and released it. The other hand grasped for something to cling to, and this action moved the unseen regulator forward. With a shudder and a solitary bark from its filthy stack, the engine began moving away from the Inspector and his men.

Ladderman jumped up from the floor, and, with a gleam in his eyes, began blowing the horn again.

Temporarily stunned, two policemen grasped for the ladders which led to the cab, but were unsuccessful. Hastli frantically waved to the ever watchful switch tender, who threw the manual lever just as he was told.

In the cab, the DOSE Club cheered in ignorance as the Peak tried to gather speed. Their glee faded as the switch tender gave them a wry smile and the engine lurched violently to the right, causing Dibble and Big Jake to fall. Dan, in a frenzy, yanked back on the regulator and applied the brake. The yard track curved sharply again and the end buffers were now clearly visible. Dan's actions saved the engine and his friends from harm; however, the Peak did strike the buffers with enough force to throw everyone else to the floor. That gave the Inspector and his men enough time to once again surround the wheezing Peak. The solitary switch tender, having repositioned the points, locked the switch and drifted off to the marshalling yardmaster's shack.

Dan shut the Peak down, turned to his fearless group, and said, "Now look, let ME do the talkin'!"

Sullen faces were his only reply.

"Come out o' that engine, afore we come *get* you out!" yelled Hastli with gusto.

Slowly, gradually, the left door of the cab creaked open, and the once proud, giddy members of the little society gingerly assembled themselves in front of the Inspector.

"Here, they're Scots! All different, too," noted one of the policemen.

"Scots? Scots! Suppose you tell me what six Scots is doin' drivin' a British Railways engine down the track, and refusin' t' stop unless you had no choice?"

"Aye. Aye aye," said Ladderman. "We're Scots. Down t' visit air long-last uncle."

"'Aye aye?' Scots? Where are you from, then?" continued Hastli.

Dibble spoke up. “Ayeeburg. Inverborough. Skye Dip Island.”

The Inspector exchanged glances with his men. Then Big Jake, the most eloquent speaker of them all, took up the challenge. Lapsing in and out of his own brogue, his ‘Scotch’ accent, and Dan’s way of speaking, he gave little reason for presumption.

“Well, sir, a bunch o’ hooligans had gathered hard by this here engine and began ’busing it, throwing things against it and all. We took it upon ourselves to chase ’em off. There were more o’ them than us, but we managed to set them off on a different course. Well, sir, here they come again, armed with brickbats, clubs, and such, so we weren’t in no position t’ defend ourselves, or save the engine. So Dan says, ‘Let’s git aboard an’ move it out the way from them all.’ So we all climb on and Ladderman here gets t’ soundin’ the horn, to… bring attention to our plight. Now Dan, likin’ diesels as he does, got them driver manuals and studies ’em real good, even ’bout them Peaks. Dan, well, he knows ’bout the controls, so he gets it out of the station, intact! Weren’t that grand? Guess he forgot about the toyme an’ where we was headed. An’ here we are, talkin’ to you.”

The ‘hooligans’ were never found. DOSE made a desultory confession to all their recent ‘escapades’, as Hastli pronounced them. MacLeish was called in the next day and identified all the men as the very ones who had made his life miserable for not one, but two days. He disabused the notion of the little band’s Scottish authenticity and declared he was glad to see them behind solid steel bars, even if one “could quote Bobby Burns pretty fair”. The judge, more in pity than anger, sentenced them all to one year in jail.

One Year Later….

It was a cool, melancholy spring morning when Dan & Co emerged from their confines. A steady driving rain soaked them clear through before they had covered the short distance from the prison gate to a waiting taxi, which took them to the nearest railway station. They vaguely agreed to meet at the Madd Dogg Inn a year later. They mumbled their breathy goodbyes and, one by one, sadly departed on their respective trains to whence they had come from. We do not know if all members were able to revive their former occupations at this juncture, but Dan, rootless vagabond that he was, arbitrarily decided to head over the border to the little Welsh village which had offered him sustenance. However, the only train available to get him there with the right connection departed at a later hour.

With characteristic indifference, Dan paid his tickets with what little remuneration he had. Once again, history was repeating itself. The train rides were uneventful, save for the odd characters who boarded and left the carriages with an air of overgrown weariness.

The engine driver, a little less merciful than was his wont, suddenly brought the train to a staggering halt at _____ Station. This had the effect of waking Dan with a jolt, and caused him to hit his head on the seat in front of him. As he peered out the grimy window, once familiar buildings and streets became painfully evident. Well, he briefly reflected, at least I haven't passed the night under a street… yet.

Once off the train, he heard church bells ringing and concluded he had nothing better to do than attend a service. But at this hour? At which church? Where? He fell in behind a small crowd of fairly well-dressed middle-aged men and women. His rootless mind told him that he should follow them to whatever church they were going.

He warily entered the dimly lit entrance. Once past the narthex which contained old lithographs of the celebrated and venerable clergy of another age, he darted across the back of the nave, selecting a pew on the far left, about two-thirds back, and sat along the aisle. It had been years since he had attended church, and he found himself taking in the structure of the building as well as the places of the choir and clergy in the chancel. Three people took their seats ahead of him, two rows up. He was aware of their presence, but only after the sermon began did Dan really notice them, and more specifically, the girl.

She was sandwiched tightly between her father on her left and her fairly well-preserved mother on her right. She was very thin, but graceful, with light brown hair which cascaded down her back halfway in sweeping ringlets. Her dress, a white floral on a medium blue, looked cool and comfortable on her, although the lack of enough material on her shoulders allowed her thin white bra straps to be seen. These she adjusted once during the sermon under Dan's watchful eyes.

Several times he saw her turn, casting furtive glances behind her. Was she looking at him, or the overly silent swarthy young man who sat in the pew behind him? Towards the very end of the service she suddenly turned and gave him a fleeting stare. The one thing about her which so clearly stood out was her eyes, a misty greenish blue which suggested something warm and inviting, like a flower bud that slowly opens under the gentle coaxing of the morning sun.

Unfortunately he could think of nothing to say or do, and merely stared in return, taken aback by the unusual beauty he never expected to find. Then he turned round himself to see some of the congregation leaving the sanctuary. When he looked back at her again, she was facing the altar. I better not bother her, he thought. She must be praying.

At the Fellowship Hall, where refreshments were served, he saw her walking in several minutes after he did. She was talking to the still overly silent swarthy young man. So had she turned to look at him in church, or had he merely been in the way? As she held a tiny cup of juice and a cookie in her slender hands, he recognized the odd way she was standing, her weight favouring one side of her body, her head slightly cocked to the same side, as a stance he sometimes favoured. It was odd to see a little bit of himself in her. This girl seemed full of surprises.

It did not occur to him until later to ask someone what her name was, and he thought about the unexpected mystery of the girl as he watched her drift off with her parents when the refreshments gave out.

Since Dan had nothing to do, he stood awkwardly, feeling the cold stares of the regulars. Now what?

An old woman approached him with a toothy grin, but Dan froze. He tried to get away from her but stepped on her big right toe with his dirty boot, which caused a yelp and the stern countenances to continue their unblinking gapes. He skulked in another corner, studying his own toes.

"I want some more tea," he mumbled to the wall. An older man motioned to him slowly from across the room. "We have more in the kitchen. Come this way."

Slowly, painfully, Dan emerged from the corner, clutching his little cup as if it were his only possession in the world (which was too close to the truth to be dismissed lightly). It took him the better part of a minute to cross the hall to where the older man was standing, waiting patiently. Perhaps he recognized Dan's predicament better than he let on. He was ushered gently into the kitchen, still complete with the original cabinetry and appliances from the 1920s. The well-worn confines of the place, along with the aromatic steaming tea, allowed Dan a heart-felt respite from all his troubles. He found a wooden high-backed chair and gratefully received another cup of the warming brew.

"Just what you need," said his new friend with a smile. All Dan could do was drink slowly and stare at the man who busied himself with the final duties of closing the kitchen down for the rest of the night. He held out his cup for more. When the last of the regulars had straggled out of the worn threshold, the remaining tea been poured into a large thermos, and the pot cleaned and dried, Dan thought it was his cue to leave as well. But the man turned to him sharply, narrowed his eyes, and enquired, "Where are you off to now?"

Dan froze again. Here he was, in yet another place, unable to provide a solid, concrete answer; no where to go, no job, no money, no kitchens to clean, or dishes to wash. He stared at his toes and studied the few cracks between the polished wooden parquet floor with great concentration.

"Ah, so it's like that, eh?" surmised his new friend by the name of Jones. "Well, young man, you've run into a bit of luck. It just so happens I've a spare room where you can stay awhile."

So with a little bounce to his step, Dan followed Jones down

Cranhill Lane, crossed the main avenue (far from the Green Dragon), and down another street where he turned suddenly to the right. A very narrow alley led them to a brightly-painted green door. Another green door, another tragic outcome, or would this be different? The door had a polished brass knocker but no green dragon. Jones quickly unlocked the stout door and motioned Dan inside.

A small set of stairs was to his right. Dan admired the carved wooden handrail, made of heavy oak. Straight on, an incapacious hallway led to a formal parlour to his left. The very small, airless dining room was seen to the right, and the yellow kitchen was farther down by a good 25 feet, or so Dan estimated.

"There be a small room off the kitchen to your left. Suppose you go in there and take a rest." Jones poured most of the tea into a large mug and disappeared into the parlour, turned its lights on, and grabbed a newspaper. Speechless, frowsy, and uncomfortable in this man's clean dwelling, Dan found the brown door to the left of the kitchen. He pushed it open cautiously. A small, cosy guest room had been tastefully furnished in period furniture. He guessed the style was at least 100 years previous. It was almost as if he had stepped back in time; the only hint of modernity was the electric lamp on the dresser, itself in the Victorian style. Even the little clock on the bed stand was a wind-up model. It made a soft ticking sound which relaxed Dan even further.

He fell on the carefully appointed bed and was asleep within five minutes. His dreams were of the girl in church, MacLeish, Scots garb, and bagpipe music.

The next morning, Dan woke up in a mental fog. For a minute he did not remember where he was, or even how he had gotten to this cosy room. The complete silence, save the little wind-up clock, unnerved him, and he felt compelled to get up. It was past nine on the clock. He stumbled into the kitchen. There was a note on the gleaming table: "Have gone out to get a newspaper. Be back shortly. Welcome, and make yourself at home." He ignored the urgent hunger pangs for the want of drink. Rummaging through the cabinets, he eventually discovered the place where Jones kept a cache of spirits. Staring at the small collection, he dismissed the Glenlivet for a bottle of Gordon's. He found a glass near the sink and put too much gin in it. An investigation into the liquid contents of the refrigerator revealed only a red, fruity 'kids-type' juice. Well, he rationalized, it's better than water. After mixing some of the juice with the gin, he drank greedily, eager to put the whole sordid mess of his life on temporary hold. Damn it all, he wanted to get good and drunk, especially on somebody else's quid, not his own. And drink he did, continuing long after the juice had been depleted. When the spirits caught up with him, he felt a sudden urge to eat. A desperate search turned up a box of biscuits, but they disintegrated in his shaky hands. Suddenly he sank to the floor and remained in a crumpled position.

Jones had been delayed by more than one gossipy parishioner, who accosted him on the street, and demanded to know what he had done "with that vagrant who drank tea like he had never tasted it before". The newspaper lorry, which normally delivered on time, was over an hour late. Hustling back to his house, he found his dazed guest attempting not to be sick on the floor, which had been cleaned only yesterday.

Jones, more disgusted than anything else, hurried him out the front door, and told him not to anticipate the charity of others "if certain advantages were expected". Dan was sick, drunk, and overly hungry. He wandered through the village in a totally aimless fashion. No one bothered him, and for that he was dimly thankful. He continued on like this for the rest of the day. He noted the passing of the long afternoon shadows being cast by the stately trees along the village heath. But in what seemed a matter of minutes, the sun had said its farewell to the western sky and once again, Dan found himself in similar circumstances, ones he preferred not to remember. A stretch of old grey slate sidewalk struck a not-so-distant bell inside him. Another groggy recollection urged him to keep walking until he found steam emanating from a vent in the walk.

With an eerie accuracy, he not only found the same opening, he remembered where the old iron bar was (behind the large dustbins) that he had used previously. The manhole cover was a welcome sight. He crawled back into the darkness, felt along the large insulated steam pipe, and located the ledge he had used before. The warmth from the pipe was a comfort to him as the ensuing evening was fast turning cool. He assumed his slouched position, and thus spent the night in warm dejection.

# CHAPTER FOUR
# The Phoenix Riseth

The old hovel was a questionable shelter from the howling winds, blowing snow, and freezing temperatures on a dark, foreboding English winter's night. A filthy archaic stove gave off a good measure of strong heat. A small lamp had been placed upon a battered wooden stool, around which sat a group of crouched figures. A decrepit excuse of a door had a life of its own, and hung precariously on a few rusted nails. It had to be barred to stay shut, and pieces of it hung like torn curtains. A denim-clad man got up and put his back to the door. The hovel began to warm up slowly. The huddle was comprised of mostly middle-aged to retired men, who should have known better than to endure their present condition.

Guilford was the acknowledged leader. Tall, a touch of silver in his hair, of medium build, he had the air of the gentleman and the savvy of the working man. His mere words were enough to encourage, inspire, quell, or mediate any situation. He provided the guiding vision to the present enterprise. (What enterprise? Read on.)

Tom, somewhere near three score, was a steam man, having served the Southern and BR until the 60s. He was extremely knowledgeable about all aspects of railway life, yet his expertise was rarely called on, or appreciated. Clad in a Southern Railway grease cap, Tom lent an air of authenticity to the group.

Clancyman had retired from the Post, lived a few miles away, and was there mainly because he could not think of anything else to do. His usual method of discourse was chiefly within the realm of complaint and dissent.

Lon, the laconic one, lolled against the tattered door, oblivious to the cold or anything. Rarely expressing any thought at all, never complaining, this unusual 36-year-old of independent means was always in denim, wore a BR grease cap, performed any requested task, yet no one was ever quite sure of what he was thinking. He was *there*.

Donald 'Doc' Mertz was yet another retired man with time on his hands until he had heard of Guilford's scheme to turn a disused scrap yard and adjacent buildings into an historical and industrial railway centre. Someone in Doc's family had once been a LSWR signalman, and so, he reasoned, he might make some contribution to the effort. Doc liked to wear plaid shirts, but bore no Scottish ancestors. He was one of the more eager of the bunch.

The subject at hand was the most up-to-date news listed in a popular publication enjoyed by rail enthusiasts. Guilford began to read.

"Listen to this. 'Famous Peak stalls on Ais Gill… the TBPPS's 'Neverfail' slipped uncontrollably on approach to Ais Gill to enthusiasts' horror. What was so difficult to ascertain was why the vintage diesel could not regain adhesion with a rake of just three carriages.'" Guffaws of laughter were then heard.

"Wot was in them carriages? Lead?" asked Tom. "Maybe they was all built like you, Doc." Dr Mertz did not appreciate the allegation or the comparison, but he kept his silence.

"Let's hear some more," said Clancyman.

Guilford turned a few leaves and read on. "Two tanks take a turn at Wiggin."

"Tanks? Aw, skip that," grumbled Tom, a former top link driver.

"Hold on there, Tom. Tankies are what we need to hear about. Tankies are cheaper than tender engines. And we got to get one. Read it," urged Doc.

"No. Tank engines ain't the way t' go. Don't 'ave enough power," continued the former driver. "I've driven both."

"Tom, even if we could afford to buy a tender engine, where are we going to run it, on our limited marshalling yard?" argued Doc.

"Ahh, ya got no vision," answered Tom, getting irritated.

"I say we get a *tank* engine. Cheaper, better, less maintenance, less coal and water. We don't even have one carriage! That old 'Toad' brake van will take months to restore, maybe longer. What do you want, Tom, a 'Brittania' or a 9F?"

"Or, 'ow 'bout a 'Schools' Class?" quarrelled Tom.

Guilford looked up from his magazine. "Quit. Mark this. 'Tank for Sale. Snakepit and Froggy Pond Railway proposes to sell its 1860s 'Fancy Stair' Well tank, so named for its elaborate iron steps to the footplate, a product of the short-lived Stickfire and Coal Loco Company Limited.'"

"Here, whoever 'eard of the Stickfire Loco Company?" laughed Tom, waving Guilford's magazine away.

"Tom, it says the company was short-lived," reminded Guilford. He continued reading. "'The engine's lack of use has led the Railway to attempt to sell the vintage loco.'"

"Stick burner? Surely they mean coal burner," said Tom critically.

"How much do they want for that piece of junk?" asked Clancyman.

"It says here that the Railway is accepting all tenders, but acknowledged that the minimum bid must be at least 150,000 quid."

"One hundred fifty thousand quid!" yelled everyone except Guilford.

"The cost of moving that old thing is going to be the next topic as the price does not include transport, if I'm not mistaken," observed Lon. Everyone was stunned by this pronouncement because Mr Lon had deigned to speak. Of course, now that he did, it was a foregone conclusion that he was not going to speak again for the rest of the evening.

"Hello, Professor," saluted Tom.

"What rock have you been hiding under, or has the wind got your ear?"

"Oh, stop it," complained old Clancyman.

"I say we buy it," said Doc with emphasis.

"A stick burner? You're crackers," laughed Tom. "I can see it now. Doc and his friends (that's one) spendin' all their time collecting sticks and firewood in the woods and by the sides of roads. But there are no woods round 'ere!"

"Think of the money we could save on coal," continued Doc. "I think one of us should go up there and buy it. We have nothing else and no other prospect at present of pulling our 'Toad'. Can you think of something better?"

"Doc's gonna be collectin' sticks," began Tom again.

"Right. Go ahead, but buy it with *your* money," replied Clancyman to Doc's question. "Who among us has 150,000 quid, or more?" He drained the last of his tea and got up, stretched and said, "I'll 'ave a look round before we go." And he left, tightening his cap in preparation for the storm, which was still active inside. Lon moved aside so he could pass out, then resumed his former position.

"Well, unless we turn up somming big or one o' you chaps wins a lottery, we can't buy the 'Fancy Stair' or anything else," moralized Tom.

Guilford turned another page. "Look, here's our bit," he said. "'Society Seeks Volunteers. The Scrap and Skull Railway is anxious to welcome new volunteers. Deep in the heart of what once was an extensive, active storage, scrap iron, steel, and warehouse district, the Society has so far taken possession of at least one mile of the former company's industrial sidings, some warehouses, storage sheds, and a donated 1904 'Toad' brake van. Why the skull? 'Well,' explained Robert Guilford, Chairman of the Society, 'one of my ancestors several generations back was reputed to have sailed with an infamous pirate in his earlier years. The railway and company which served this area were both in existence for over 100 years before ceasing operation.' The Society is located downline from Bonehead Scrappers within easy walking distance of Factory Furnace Station. If you arrive at Inchey's Scrap Yard, you have gone too far.'"

"Well, let's hope it brings some results," sighed Doc, mindful of the hour.

With that, the men bade each other good night, and wended their respective ways to warmer and cosier surroundings. Clancyman waited until they left, and carefully locked the gates with what appeared to be a relic itself. The gate to the permanent way was kept locked, as there was no traffic, and had not been for some time. But Clancyman had the key to that gate as well. Would it ever be used again?

Meanwhile as they pondered the stability of Doc's inner faculties, safe and warm in their flats or homes, a forlorn figure stood in a dark alley in a little Welsh village whose name most Englishmen could never hope to pronounce. Dan's appointed hour for rummaging through dustbins was at hand. Sometimes he was lucky. He well remembered the night when some careless, overstuffed diner had tossed out a plate full of spaghetti, still warm on its white take-away plate. Usually he had to make do with scraps and what the restaurants threw out after eleven, or later.

But Diesel Dan's luck was holding out: more than unwanted chips and bits of fish tails this night! Someone had actually thrown away a well-known enthusiasts' publication (food for *mental* thought). He delved into the garbage and found a gloomy street lamp to peruse his new-found treasure. A wan light was all he could garner, but it was all that was needed. Dan held the magazine up towards the light. A mention of a certain railway, newly formed (within a year), and in want of volunteers caught his eye. A strange, hazy idea began to eddy around Dan's already addled mind… join the bunch of 'suckers', secure a shed for Deltic parts, build the Deltic again when no one was looking… and dandy as candy… a perfect plan! Now his mind attempted to run with the 'facts'; time to call the faithful together, hatch the scheme, enlist his members, and get on with it!

Dan placed the magazine in a back trouser pocket. He rummaged again, found a half-eaten Chinese-type dinner (in Wales, he wanted to know?), and gobbled while he schemed in back of a black, smelly dustbin.

The first thing in the morning was to telegraph his DOSE members and urge them to return to the Madd Dogg Inn in Blue-Ped-on-Riveredge that very Saturday for 'Urgent Business'. The rest of the week was spent relieving himself in the heath bushes, eating leftover dinners from dustbins, begging beer and other spirits (but nowhere near the Green Dragon or that church), and scheming. His secret residence continued to serve him well. But he made sure that the manhole cover was firmly in place once the rumble of wheels alerted him to the dawn of yet another day. He did not see HenWas or Brynn that week. Had he forgotten the brothers came to the village once a week, and not on the same day? No one had ever disturbed him under the street. Who would be crawling under there at night anyway?

The only problem which really bothered him was how to get to the Madd Dogg Inn. He went to the BR station, 'stole' a timetable (he did not know they were free), and furtively looked up the departures and connections. After making a desultory visit to the ticket clerk, he determined that the sum needed to complete the purchase was clearly beyond his means. The Madd Dogg Inn was too far to walk on foot. After all, it was in England! How then? Dan had a suspicion of asking for rides from the street. A strange, hazy idea eddied around his already addled mind. But for once, this one had merit.

Dan had long noted the craze for antiques, and resolved to raid the village dump for old bottles. He smeared grease on them with butter and bacon drippings from "Fannie's Breakfast Nook's" dustbins, let them dry in the sun, stashed them behind one of the large dustbins near his manhole, called them 'antiquities', and hawked them outside the 'bus depot and food market. By Friday he had 'earned' over 244 pounds, more than enough for the tickets, and plenty to spare. So after selling the very last of the bottles, and collecting a premium price for each one, he gleefully headed to the station, purchased his tickets, stole two hamburgers off a tray in the Wimpy Bar, took three bottles of ale from an unsuspecting pensioner, scared an old woman into giving him a bottle of gin ("Here, I seed you round the corner last night wi' that big bloke. Strange if yer 'usband should find out…"), headed back 'home', and consumed the lot, content to sleep it off.

After relieving himself for the last time that morning behind his favourite bush, he stumbled in the direction of the station. A short blast of a passing BR diesel caused him to quicken his formerly cautious pace. When he arrived, he attempted to stare at the clock with bleary eyes, and reasoned that he had not long to wait until the time of departure.

Fifteen minutes later Dan was out of town, scheming away while his fellow passengers remarked about his general appearance, his dire need of a shave, bath, clean clothes, etc. Dan was so involved he did not notice who or what was going on as the carriage became less and less populated. Several hours later found him on the threshold at the Madd Dogg Inn.

"Here now, this be a respectable place," protested the barmaid at the sight of the dishevelled customer. Dan, however, was well prepared for this. He had hidden most of his money in various pockets. Inside two wrapped banknotes, he had placed a wad of newspaper to make it seem as if he had more than was noticeable at first.

He began waving his 'money' around, saying, "Look, girlie, I got money t' spend."

Dan was regretfully shown to the same sparse and small back room where he had held court one year ago. After ordering fish, chips, and plenty of ale, he settled down to wait for the faithful to arrive. Odd that no one had replied to his fevered telegrams….

It was late afternoon when Ladderman threw open the door to the small, dingy back room and found Dan slumped over the table, surrounded by the empty plate and too many bottles of ale.

"Well, look at you. Look like you've been in the streets your whole life."

Slowly, painfully, Dan opened his eyes. The figure of a very tall and angry man began to take form. Ladderman looked like he had come straight from the dairy farm, which he had, not even bothering to change clothes.

"Ladderman, right…. Where are the others?"

"We've all been on the telephone, saying we're not goin' chasin' round the country for some stupid plan. We already did that twice now, and look at the trouble you got us into! And furthermore… most of them had to beg to get their jobs back! Don's not coming, nor Dibble, Big Jake, or Bob Brake!"

Ladderman, of course, was referring to the prison sentences DOSE received as a result of the 'Scotch Kilt Scheme'. Dan finally managed to look Ladderman in the face. He was not a happy man.

"Are you listening? I repeat, Oily Oil won't lose his job *again*, Big Jake isn't taking time from work. Nor will Dibble or Bob Brake. We're not spending any time in Her Majesty's Prison for your stupid ideas! I'm appointed to say it to your face!"

But Dan, hazy as his mind was, knew Ladderman's weakness: alcohol. He ordered more ale and got Ladderman terribly drunk. Then he persuaded him that *this* was a fool-proof plan. The angry owner, who demanded they pay their bill after discovering them rolling empty ale bottles on the floor and betting which one would strike the door first, grabbed them by their necks and hurled them out the stout oaken door. They tumbled into the street, much to the amusement of the nearby pedestrians. Dazed and confused, they got up and wavered along the sidewalk, not knowing where they were headed. Dan had a knack for finding alleys and dustbins, and nudged Ladderman into a narrow one hard by the Inn. Ladderman had no intention of sleeping near a dustbin. He had brought along some emergency cash, in case of some unforeseen situation. But Dan got him to agree – mostly likely with the idea of saving money. Still, Ladderman, aware he was nearly out of control of himself, clung hard to the notion that he would not let Dan find the cash he had brought along.

After finding a suitable location, they quickly dozed off, more in thanks to the bottles of ale than the spot itself.

"Here ya, yon beggars, be gone with ya!" An angry woman was swinging a broom, raining down blows upon the drowsy heads of our two friends, rousing them to an uneasy realization that (1) morning had broken; (2) someone nearby was not pleased with their choice of accommodation. They moved off slowly, but with effort. Ladderman, for once being the brighter of the two, headed towards the railway station; Dan followed five steps behind. "I've got enough for us t' get t' London and that other station (Factory Furnace)." Dan was happy to allow him to pay for both fares, smiling to himself as they prepared to board.

The dishevelled demeanour of the two men kept their company amongst themselves, as the rest of the occupants of their carriage moved away or found suitable seats elsewhere.

Euston seemed to have not changed much, but Dan observed that more youth appeared lolling round, and they did not look or act like trainspotters. The ride to Factory Furnace Station was, in some ways, painful for both. That station was one of the former scenes of their melodramatic attempts to salvage the now lost Deltic….

On their way to the Scrap and Skull, they had to pass Bonehead Scrappers, and remembrances of former failures there led them to hang their heads low as they passed the same battered gate and the watchman's shack, where the old Scot, still on duty, studied them with a curious eye.

"Could it be? Och, no, not *them*." Something caused him to stare until they were out of his sight. Then the telephone rang and he became distracted.

Oh, what a sad and weary walk that was for 'Diesel Dan' Settles and Jacob Jonathan Ladderman. Scenes of former disasters kept snapping at their dirty boot heels like angry dogs. Why oh why couldn't it have been different?

It was late afternoon when the imposters staggered into the area owned by the Scrap and Skull. Dan tried the main gate to the road but found it padlocked. Another locked gate, another disaster? Not this time! In anger and despair mixed with weariness he shook the fence, which jangled the gate. A sprightly old man suddenly appeared.

"Here, lads, can y' read the sign? 'Closed until further notice.'" Clancyman turned away but Ladderman was not going to be dismissed so easily.

"Bouonjour. Be this the Skull an' Crossbones Rail—" An elbow into his side did not permit him to continue his question.

“Scrap an’ Skull! First you called it the ‘Skull an’ Scar’, now this! I’ll do the talkin’ remember?”

Clancyman turned to face them. “No, it’s the Scrap and Skull,” he said testily.

“Where’s the Chairman o’ this place? Those sheds belong t’ you? Where’s the snack shop, hobby store, tools, an’ such?” queried Dan hurriedly.

“Hold on there! Who are you an’ yer misinformed companion?” asked Clancyman slowly.

“My name is Dan Settles; this is my trusted friend Jacob Jonathan Ladderman. We’re from that famous Birmingham preserved railway.” Dan thought that would be enough to get them in the gate.

“Wot’s that then? Never been up that way.”

“Why, man, where ’ave you been?” shouted Dan.

“Well, I liked t’ take the ‘Brighton Belle’ down south in the summer.”

“We’re from that famous railway… the… Kickcloth and Seamside,” Dan said, making up a name quickly as he thought of the once great mills of England that supplied the world. “I’m Chief Loco Inspector; Ladderman is almost a passed cleaner and… jack of all trades.”

“Really? Why then ’ave you travelled all the way from the Kickclothing t’ see us?”

“Well… we were recently given an official leave of absence to give you a hand in your start-up,” explained Ladderman.

“Start-up? We’ve been ’ere for eight months,” advised Clancyman.

Dan felt like kicking Ladderman but chose diplomacy instead. “We read in *Railway Review* that your Society needed volunteers. After discussing your situation with our… Board of Directors, they decided that they could spare us for a while. So, ’ere we are.”

“An’ we can stray until March,” added Ladderman, despite a step on his big right toe by Dan. “Just need to make a call en Jerri.”

“‘Stray?’ You mean, stay? On official leave?”

“Right. Now, where’s the warehouses an ’such that you own?”

“Hold on.” Clancyman pulled out an impressive steel ring with many keys, some ancient and thicker than a man's thumb, others shiny and small. The padlock and chain gave way to a gravel road littered with coal and bits of iron and steel here and there. He led them round the venerable buildings as Dan noted they had stumbled upon a hodge-podge of abandonment, probably gotten for a song. Beyond that, he spotted a water column, some outbuildings and sheds, and a weathered van on one of many tracks. A hut that looked suspiciously familiar in its construction stood near a tool shed and behind that was a tiny loo with a few extra plumbing features. Smoke curled out of the hut invitingly.

"Where's the engine shed?" wondered Dan, his eyes darting to and fro, with a scheme already built in his addled mind.

"None. Got a 1904 'Toad' brake van hereabouts… on that track. No engine shed. But them sheds' got tracks which lead inside 'em." Dan was pleased to hear that bit of news. He saw the hand-thrown switch levers and smiled to himself.

Ladderman, however, was not impressed, and began laughing. "I suppose you could call yourselves 'The Scrap Pile'."

Clancyman stopped walking. "I'll pretend I didn't 'ear that."

Dan saw his chance to impress. "You shouldn't. He often talks without thinkin' first." Ladderman wanted to cuff him for that, but did not follow through.

"What are these fellows doing here?" enquired Guilford, seeing Clancyman with the strangers.

"These 'fellows' are from some Society in Birmingham on a leave of absence to volunteer with us," filled in Clancyman.

"Welcome to the Scrap and Skull," said Guilford warmly.

"Thank you," answered Dan, shaking his hand. "We're glad t' be 'ere."

"First thing is… you better quit calling it the 'Scrap an' Skull'," advised Ladderman, looking round at the dismal conditions, then shaking hands with Guilford and Clancyman.

"Oh? Well what should we call it, Mr—"

"Ladderman, almost a passed cleaner, and jack. Chein qu j'di'te a faithe."

"Ah, a man from the Jersey Isle. Bouonjour."

"Looks like that name run everybody off. Might 'ave scared 'em."

"I think we ought t' warm ourselves by the fire in the hut," offered Clancyman. "I'm getting cold." An icy wind was cutting across the yard, and he was not the only one who felt its chill. The four men went inside the shack and sat down near the filthy but hot stove. Gusts of wind whistled through the flimsy door.

"Somebody better give that thing a good cleaning," observed Ladderman, pointing to the stove.

"I'll get some steel wool and rags, and let you get started on it in the morning," responded Guilford seriously. Ladderman nodded his head in response. But then he continued, "That 'door' doesn't keep much cold out. Somebody should—"

"There will be tools and plenty of wood for that also," added Guilford. Dan glowered at Ladderman, daring him to say anything else. Ladderman took the hint and kept quiet. Doc made some notations and disappeared.

That evening, Dan presented his and Ladderman's dubious credentials to the Society by using a hastily scrawled letter on plain stationery signed with illegible signatures. This had been done in a railway carriage with some 'borrowed' paper from an unsuspecting passenger's tote bag. Luckily, no one had been to Birmingham lately, or knew anything of the railfan activity (or lack of it) at the Kickcloth and Seamside, the city's best kept secret, which was swallowed hook, line, and sinker. The new volunteers spent the night in the staff hut, wrapped in thick woollen blankets.

The next morning Dan and Ladderman were awakened by the steady shouts of labourers. The stove had grown cold, but the sun shone brightly, and the icy wind was gone. A peek out of the decrepit door revealed all the Scrap and Skullers hard at work on a derelict-looking wooden shed. One side was in dire need of replacement, the boards nearly rotted through in places. The men were pulling them down with some vigour, Doc leading them with words of encouragement. A few men were on ladders, calling to others before the loosed boards clattered to the ground.

Ladderman roused himself and saw the steel wool, rags, bucket of water, wood, tools, and screws. Dan found a tea pot on a metal stand. He poured himself a cup while Ladderman hummed an obscure tune, scouring the stove.

"Mmm. Tea's hot enough to wake you up."

"I'm awake. When was the last time this poor thing was ever cleaned? What's all that racket out there in the bel? Hmm… looks like they're destroyin' one o' their own buildings, it does." But Ladderman could not clearly see what was really going on, due to the cloudy windows and his crouched position on the floor. "Je' c'mench 'chons."

Dan had just finished his tea and that remark jolted him into action. Sheds, or at least one, were part of his plan! Dan burst out the door, nearly tearing it from its hinges, and ran headlong over to the busy workers.

"Here, now, wot's the idea? Tearin' down the shed?" wailed Dan.

"Why, friend, you seem all in a tizzy! Very strange, I dare say. Mightn't you had a bad dream last night?"

Dan recalled last night's witless dream where bagpipe music had been heard and kilt-clad men walked in time to the music. MacLeish was at the head of them. He tried to shake it off. This was not the first time he had suffered through that dream.

"That 'pears t' 'ave only rot on one side, Mr Guilford. Why tear the whole thing down?" continued Dan, almost in tears.

"Friend, friend, you mistake us. You must have quite an appreciation for historic buildings! Well, well, I do say you'll make a *fine* volunteer. As you pointed out, three-quarters of the building is sturdy and well. We are removing the siding on this section and will replace it with the wood you see over there." He pointed to a pile of boards stacked up against a battered zinc building which served as the tool shed. "Doc has already measured and cut them to size."

"Phew! You really 'ad me worried," sighed Dan, calming down.

"Care to join us now?"

"Allow me another cup of tea an' we'll be right with you. Ladderman's cleaning the stove as we speak."

"Fair enough." Guilford picked up his crowbar and began prying off the same piece he had started on before Dan had startled him to a standstill.

Dan made his way back to the hut, muttering to himself, "No wonder they call this the *Scrap* Railway." Ladderman had just completed the first job he was given, and the old stove shone like freshly polished silver plate. Dan was taken aback by the transformation. Ladderman rinsed the rags, returned, and reached for the last of the tea before Dan could get his second cup. But there was enough for him as he poured the last of the strong brew.

Ladderman proceeded to dismantle what was left of the door and salvaged the handles, lock, and hinges. Doc must have measured and sawed these pieces too, for in less than 30 minutes Ladderman had fashioned a nearly new door, screwed the handles and lock in place, secured it on its hinges, and tested it by opening and shutting it several times. Dan was speechless. Ladderman hummed that obscure tune again while he oiled the hinges and then cleaned up.

Fortified with tea and determination where the sheds were concerned, Dan and his friend approached Guilford, albeit a little too closely. The board Guilford was extricating sprang forward, striking Dan on the side of his head, and knocking him down.

Ladderman shouted, "Is that any way t' treat the Inspector, eh?" But the Scrap band instantly broke into laughter while Ladderman continued to fume.

Tom walked over to Dan. "Serves ya right, getting so close." He extended a hand to Dan. Guilford quickly took charge.

"Seeing as you're a little skittish round here today, might you get all these old boards and put them over there?" He pointed to a space that was once a coal heap and the zinc tool shed. "See those axes there? Separate the boards, decide what we can use for the stove, and break it up into usable pieces. Put the good ones in that little shed. Throw the rest into those dustbins." He pointed to the main gate area.

"Is that any way t' treat the Inspector, eh?" repeated Ladderman. But no one was paying attention to him.

"Good idea," mouthed Dan. "As cold as it is, we'll need something to burn in there."

So Dan and Ladderman laboriously stacked the old boards between the former coal heap and the metal tool shed as they received them. They then ascertained which pieces could be saved, and broke up the usable sections into pieces that would fit the old wood- or coal-burning stove. Ladderman hauled the unusable sections to the industrial size dustbins near the road. When Doc attempted to suggest a more efficient procedure, Guilford held up his hand and waved him off, reasoning that they had their own peculiar method. This occupied them as the others removed the old sections and replaced them with a strange amount of precision, led by Doc.

Guilford called the work to a halt at 3:30. Soon afterwards a small van went past the gate, blew its horn, and Dan saw a brown parcel fly over the fence. Clancyman went to retrieve it and the men put their tools in the shed and headed towards the staff hut. They stopped to admire Ladderman's efforts. Lon whistled with approval and the men clapped Ladderman on the back. As they entered the hut, they were momentarily blinded as the sun struck the now cleaned and polished stove, which gleamed as if brand new. Their glowing admiration gave way to Ladderman receiving warm handshakes and thanks. Clancyman looked at the door and stove with favour as he entered the hut with the parcel. Soon they were munching on stale biscuits, scones, and rolls. Once the tea was made by Clancyman, everyone eagerly downed his share.

"That bakery down the way always gives us the leftover and sometimes a treat or two," explained Doc to the new recruits.

"I know the owner," said Guilford.

"Seems as if everything round 'ere is *scrap*," muttered Dan.

"Wot was that?" asked Tom.

"I *said*, seems like you know 'ow t' make do," answered Dan quickly.

“We ’ave to,” said Tom. “This ’ere is strictly all volunteer. Why, even the wood we’re usin’ t’ fix the shed was given to us.”

“And who was that?” asked Ladderman.

“The watchman at Bonehead Scrappers. If he finds somming they won’t sell, he contacts us. The wood we got came from inside an old parcels van. It was just sittin’ in there. Somebody just left it. Good condition, too.”

“We know that old coot. We—” But Ladderman never finished his sentence. One of Dan’s elbows had caught him in a strategic place, and he hastily withdrew from continuing.

“’E means we saw that old bloke on the way ’ere yesterday,” explained Dan quickly. “We know wot ’e looks like.”

“Got to paint the door,” ruminated Ladderman.

“Paint’s in the shed,” advised Doc. Ladderman nodded. “I’ll do it in the morning, if it’s not too cold.”

Tom continued, “He looks out for us. Gets us all kinds of things.”

“Well, if he is so generous, and that’s odd for a Scot, why doesn’t he give us that old parcels van you spoke of?” Ladderman had everyone’s attention with that question. Guilford began to look thoughtful as the little group pondered the thought.

“’Ow d’ya know he’s a Scot?” asked Clancyman.

“Aw, ’e were walkin’ round, singin’ ‘Meg on the Side o’ the Hill.’ I recognize that as some Scotch poem,” said Dan, quickly again.

“So, you read poetry?”

“Say, Tom, did MacLeish say when they were scheduled to scrap it?” Guilford turned to Tom for the answer.

“No, ’e didn’t. ’E said, ‘Come get this wood afore somebody else.’”

“Well, why not ask him? We need more than that ‘Toad’ we got on the track out there.”

“Shouldn’t be sitting out in the weather,” observed Ladderman.

Dan began to look hopeful. Another strange, hazy idea began to eddy around Dan’s already addled mind. But it began to make sense, the more he let it have free rein.

"Ladderman's right. We might be able t' get it for a reasonable price."

"We already got the 'Toad'. Needs to be put inside," repeated Ladderman.

"No, not the 'Toad'! The parcels van!"

"We got no money," complained Clancyman.

"Then we'll *get* the money," said Dan prophetically.

"How do you propose that?" asked Guilford.

"I'm thinkin'.... Lads, wot's the name o' this place?"

Clancyman answered wearily, "The Scrap and Skull. This 'ere line used to haul scrap iron and steel, an' the skull—"

"I know. The skull is about them pirates. *That's* where the money's gonna come from."

"Oh, this is good. Digging for buried treasure?" Clancyman was not interested.

"In a sense, it is. We'll use that angle t' get 'em in here."

"Get who in here?"

"Payin' customers. 'Ere's wot we do. Get all that scrap coal raked up round 'ere where it should be, in that place near the tool shed. Get an old steamship trunk, somebody go to Collector's Corner in Euston, pick up an old lantern or somming, 'ave our good friend Ladderman 'ere (clapping him on the back) dress up like a pirate, 'ave 'im stand on the coal pile next t' the trunk. Offer a chance t' get the 'buried treasure', buy a ticket an' take a number, an' the lucky man gets the 'treasure' in the steamship trunk!"

"You're crackers," complained old Clancyman.

"Got a better idea, old man?" retorted Dan, using a favourite line of his (which usually worked in certain situations).

"Well… no. But it's no good."

Doc looked hopeful as well. "I say let's try it. What do you say, Bill?"

"First, complete the shed side. Then we can try Dan's scheme."

Once the shed was completed and some primer applied on a warm afternoon, Guilford set the scheme in motion. He went to procure a pirate outfit from Maud's Emporium, then placed several ads in the enthusiasts' press advertising an 'Open Day' (with a chance at buried treasure). He ordered Doc to superintend a general clean-up of the place. Ladderman primed the door the same warm afternoon. He thoughtfully took it upon himself to rake up the footpaths and road ways, curiously separating the coal he found from the dirt, bits of iron, and trash. He did this while the others were engaged in largely removing trash and debris from the site. By Friday the coal pit not only contained a respectable pile of the same, it was neatly enclosed on three sides, the open one facing the newly cleaned gravel path. He was putting the last few nails in place as Tom and Clancyman were returning from yet another trip to the dustbins. Tom stopped to look.

"Quite 'andy by the looks o' things," he said approvingly. He called to the others. "Take a look, lads!" The rest came over to inspect Ladderman's labours.

"Where'd ja get all that coal?" asked Clancyman skeptically.

"Raked it up. There's more behind Shed No 4. Now we don't need t' buy any."

"Where'd ja get that wood?"

"From the shed. Too good t' burn, too good t' throw away."

"That wood's meant t' warm us. It's still winter, you know," complained Clancyman.

"Well, now there's coal as well."

"You've done good work, Ladderman," said Guilford. "And it shows you've got initiative. We need more men like this!"

Ladderman began to smile, feeling good about himself, and in the eyes of others, which did not come every day. Let's see… I've done the heating stove, the door, some walkways, and now the coal pile… Smartly fenced in….

"I told you blokes, Ladderman's a fine worker," chimed in Dan. "'E really puts 'imself into his tasks."

"Then 'e kin try on that pirate outfit," reminded Tom.

"Right. Com in t' the hut, warm yerself, an' try on the duds," urged Dan. But Ladderman grabbed the pirate outfit and went inside the loo to try it on.

Once everyone's tools were stowed away, hands washed, the tea and biscuits consumed, the fire again built up and enough rest had been taken by all, Ladderman emerged, complete with billowing black trousers, tall black boots, oversized coat, three-cornered hat, one gold earring, a black eye patch, and a replica sword thrust in his large belt. He looked every inch a pirate.

"Will you look there!"

"A pirate of the Spanish Main!"

"Here, mind that sword don't stick me or anybody," warned old Clancyman. And so it continued, until all present, except Dan and Ladderman, left for home. No one was willing to give them a place to live while they were at the Scrap and Skull, and the two were unwilling to part with their limited funds which they had hidden from each other. So they resigned themselves to living in the staff hut, and had been calling it home every night. Still, it wasn't too awful. The blankets were thick, the fire was warm, and the door was now secure and tight. Some donated clothing and bath essentials lay in a box. Ladderman had moved his tooth brush, toothpaste, soap, cloths, towels, and shaving needs to the loo, where a little storage cabinet kept most items. The towels were hung on a peg next to a makeshift shower. Dan kept his kit in the staff hut, fearing that someone would steal them while using the loo. Tins of beef, soup, tuna, and chicken sat on a small refrigerator, along with a box of cereal, tea, and coffee. Inside the refrigerator was milk and orange juice. Two warming plates sat on the same table as the kettle and tea pot. Several cooking pots were hanging on nails. A few forks, knives, and spoons were placed in a small tray under the warming plates. Bowls and dishes were seen above the metal stand on a small shelf. A radio was plugged into an outlet for news and amusements. Guilford had seen that the other members provide for the newcomers.

Friday brought good news. Tom had been over to Bonehead Scrappers to enquire after the parcels van. MacLeish had contacted the private owner, who had bought the van from BR, then decided he didn't want it. MacLeish said that since a 'Charity Organization' was interested, Bonehead would take 500 pounds for it, but "They only got 'til month's end, and then it's scrapped." Guilford made a call to an unknown party that afternoon.

A general meeting was held that night in the hut. Wind swirled round the buildings, trying to shake the hut, and reminded everyone it was still winter. Tom threw some more wood into the stove and made himself a cup of tea. Everyone watched him intently.

"Put that kettle on again," said Lon. Tom obliged. Soon everyone was enjoying a cup along with Tom.

Guilford rose up to speak, setting his cup down. "Right. This meeting of the Scrap and Skull Railway is called to order." He banged his fist on the wall and began. "The paths are all cleaned up. We have finished putting the new siding on Shed No 3, thanks to a good team effort. Ladderman here got us some needed improvements to our staff hut (a clean stove and a better door), a new storage area for coal, and did a nice job fencing it in. He has drawn up plans for sheds we haven't worked on, which gives us some guidelines for the future. We have done a lot, but a lot more needs to be done. Always it seems more and more. Now we have the opportunity to purchase a former BR parcels van at Bonehead Scrappers."

"Ladderman's idea," reminded Dan.

"Quite right. Mr Ladderman, we are so glad to have you. I don't see how that society in Birmingham is doing without you."

"'Twas my idea t' come 'ere," said Dan testily.

"By the by, wot's the name o' that line? I've forgotten," said Tom.

"Oh, that's the Birds—" Ladderman felt an elbow, and went on no further.

"The Kickcloth an' Seamside," said Dan quickly.

"An' how long 'ave you two been there?" continued Tom, lighting his pipe.

"Kickcloth, well, that's wot tents is made of," said Dan, trying to veer the question away. "They say if you was t' kick it, it wouldn't rip or let rain in, or tear. People began callin' it such, an' the name stuck."

"Shows one that names 'ave some meaning," nodded Clancyman.

"We're getting away from the subject at hand. For us to get that van, we've got to raise 300 pounds by the end of the month. Our generous benefactor has stated that if we do indeed raise it, he will contribute the difference. So we must show some spirit and do our best."

"Wot money do we 'ave now? An' who is this mysterious fellow?" requested Dan guardedly.

"Someone who prefers to remain anonymous. I *can* tell you he pays the taxes on the land and allows us to make a go of the place. I bring the tea, we supply your basics, tools belong to their owners or were donated, as well as just about everything else we have. We do own the 'Toad'. And, to answer your first question, not much." Guilford's keen eyes were on Dan, who began to squirm.

"I went to Collector's Corner in Euston and found two lanterns," said Lon off-handedly.

"Splendid! Anyone get a trunk yet?"

"Found one in me brother's attic," answered Clancyman. "I stowed it in the tool shed."

"Great. Then we're set for Saturday. John, open the gate at 12:00 sharp. Everybody know their places? John Clancyman at the gate, Lon Langley collect admission, Doc Mertz at the concessions, Dan Settles collect for the raffle, Jacob Ladderman help Doc Mertz and be our Captain, and I'll give the tours with Tom Masters."

"This is a hare-brained scheme if I ever 'eard one," complained Clancyman.

"Think positive!" urged Dan.

"We'll continue the general clean-up tomorrow," finished Guilford.

Saturday dawned cloudy and grey, temperature in the 40s and no precipitation. The little band of volunteers gave the place a once-over, then waited until 12:00, when Clancyman promptly swung the gate open to an empty road and sidewalk. The nearest connecting train at Factory Furnace to their opening was the 12:05. A brisk walk would get one to the Scrap and Skull within 30 minutes or less, but most people would not be in much of a hurry. Imagine the surprise when a few score enthusiasts descended on Clancyman and Lon all at once! Busily collecting admission and stamping the backs of hands with an original S&S Railway stamp donated to Guilford by the mysterious benefactor (a distant cousin), Lon could not stop to count how many passed through the gate. But Tom, temporarily standing by, did. Groups were organized by Guilford and later Tom, and their tours included some time spent on the origin and history of the railway and company, as well as the original purposes and uses of each building, with the research having been done by Guilford himself. Word got round that the tea was oddly good, and Doc did a land sale business, selling each large cup for 25 pence. Snacks went for the same price. The 'Toad' seemed to receive the lion's share of the photograph-taking, and more than a few of the enthusiasts were heard to remark that is was in fairly good shape. However, concern was voiced about leaving it to the mercy of the elements. "You need to get it out of the weather," advised one man from Devon. "Run it into that shed over there, and speedily. Your 'Toad' is definitely salvageable." Word was passed for him to meet Ladderman, who was helping Doc with concessions.

"Thanks for putting in a good word for my side," said Ladderman. "I been tellin' 'em that a few times. Make sure Guilford hears you say that." Guilford got the same advice on the next tour.

The next wave arrived at 2:30. This time Lon was ready, and the tours were arranged quicker this time round. By 4:00 little knots of friends collected together to discuss their own news and the prospects of the Scrap and Skull. At 4:15 Ladderman ducked out of the staff hut, clad in his pirate suit, strode over to the coal pile on his long legs, clamped one foot securely on the side of the steamship trunk, while balancing on the other. He surveyed the crowd with a fearful eye. A silent crowd began to circle around him.

*"Fifteen men on a dead man's chest,*
*Yo ho ho an' a bottle o'rum."*

"I've been 'cross the seven seas and found many a treasure! Davey

Jones's locker holds a special one for the lucky man who wins the drawing!" He pointed his sword at various enthusiasts. "Who will it be… you… you… or you? While I had to labour for my treasure, you can have it just by taking a chance. My Matey Dan here will tell you how!" He glared at the enthusiasts, who were spellbound.

"Right, you 'eard the Captain. Take a chance at some real treasure! Tickets, five pound. In this ol' trunk lies somming every one o' you would love t' 'ave. Take a chance, lads!"

Ladderman's deep voice and antics had the right effect, and a queue instantly formed behind Dan, who was ready. After the last ticket was sold, the Captain deftly flicked the locks down with his sword, but did not open the trunk. "All right, Matey, give us one now!" he bellowed. Dan rummaged round the little box which held all the ticket stubs and drew one out. He held it up and shouted, "Number 37!" The Captain opened the trunk and pulled out a vintage lantern. A gasp went through the throng as an elderly gent made his way to the front of the coal pile and claimed his prize, handing Dan his ticket. As he held his treasure for all to see, a wave of approval was palpable by the instant applause he received.

"Bless my soul, I've been wanting one of these for years," smiled the new owner. "And it's a Midland!" The crowd cheered heartily.

"Thank you, Captain, and thank you all for coming. We hope to see you again soon!" said Guilford enthusiastically. "We were glad to have you as our guests, and have a safe journey home!"

There was plenty of time to make the 5:50 out of Factory Furnace, and so the enthusiasts departed, with Clancyman securing the property, which included locking all the sheds down. Now it was time to count the fees. A whistling tea kettle welcomed him inside the staff hut.

"Is there enough for us?"

"Of course. We didn't use our own."

"Well, Lon, how are we in terms—"

"Jus' tell us 'ow much."

"Tom, wot was yer count?"

"By the by, first crowd came in, noisy lot, 66. Second, 48; this make a total of 114."

"Can you believe it? And this our first open day." Doc was incredulous.

"On admission, we got 228 pounds, concessions 50 pounds, and 200 for the raffle!" Guilford had tallied and written the figures down in columns inside a slim brown notebook.

"Our first open afternoon," corrected Clancyman, stirring his tea as he sat down.

"There's costs: pirate suit, concessions, lanterns. 'Ow much did that take away?" Dan was doing some figuring of his own.

"The pirate outfit is out of my own pocket," said Guilford. "It wasn't much. Maybe we should think about buying it instead of renting it. Doc got the concessions. Lon brought in the lanterns, and Clancyman put the trunk back in the tool shed for future use."

"That scheme worked well, with Ladderman as Captain," mused Doc.

"Aye. Aye aye!"

"'Aye aye?' Are you still in character, or did you serve in Her Majesty's Navy?" asked Tom.

"No. One of my brothers did that, then came back to the farm," replied Ladderman, with Dan watching every syllable. "We got a dairy."

"So, 'ave we got enough t' buy the parcels van?"

"Yes," answered Guilford, "and some left over! I'll wire our benefactor tomorrow with the good news! We brought in 478 pounds."

"Four hundred seventy-eight pounds!"

"We need to return that costume, and tell them to reserve it for us in a month or two. The other lantern is in the trunk. I am very impressed with the way everything turned out. So I won't minimize the success we've had, and a special thanks goes to Dan for the fund-raising suggestion." Guilford shook Dan's hand, who was basking in the joy of accomplishment.

"I told you blokes it'd work," Dan said quickly.

"Then we did good." Ladderman grabbed another biscuit.

"Quite right. But 'though we did well, we still need to find out the switching charge. Remember that van has to move on BR metals to get here."

"Wot's that? Why that old coot—"

"Ladderman, There you go again," admonished Clancyman.

"BR will charge us for moving the van out of Bonehead Scrappers down the line to our property and onto a chosen track," explained Guilford. "And I don't know how much that will be."

"Switching charge."

"Here, we got extree pound," said Dan.

"Not enough for the charge," counselled Tom.

"So find out."

"First things first. Ladderman, since it was your idea of getting the van, I think you should represent us in this upcoming transaction. MacLeish'll have the paperwork ready in a few days. All you do is present the cheque, which I will have the bank draw up, and he'll hand you the title and Bill of Sale." Guilford took a sip of tea.

"Can he do that?"

"Yes, he can act for us."

Ladderman gave Dan a look of panic. Dan acknowledged it by screwing up his face.

"Ah, well… I can't do that," said Ladderman haltingly.

"Why not?"

"Well, ah… I'm not quite finished mending the roof on Shed No 1. And… we got to get that 'Toad' out of the weather."

"It can wait a day or two," persuaded Lon.

"I think… what Ladderman may be saying is… he feels an 'lected officer o' this Club should be 'andling business," put in Dan at just the right time.

"Bill, 'e may 'ave a point there. MacLeish don't know this fellow." Tom did not realize the jam he might be saving Ladderman from. "Tell you what. I'll go up there and make the call to BR. Maybe I kin get 'em t' waive the charge."

"Well, 'ow kin you do that?"

"He knows all kinds of people at BR," explained Guilford. "If Tom can't get them to do anything for us, not even Sir Peter Parker could."

"Since when is you an' 'lected officer? Mr Guilford 'ere is the Chair—"

"Oh, MacLeish knows me. We served in the war together. Don't need Mr Guilford for that," assured Tom.

That Monday morning, Guilford gave everyone their assignments for the day, plus one over and above the daily tasks: move the 'Toad' into Shed No 2. It was in reasonably good condition and had a strong roof. But he did not tell them *how* to get it in there. Without delay, he left the yard on the way to the bank with the gate clanging shut behind him.

Meanwhile, the creaking wooden and metal-clad doors of Shed No 2 were thrown open, with Ladderman fetching some oil to lubricate the ageing iron hinges. The hand brake was released, and three men put their backs against it, Ladderman joining them. But it would not budge. Tom and Clancyman stood by.

"Yer crackers if you think you can move that thing," admonished Clancyman.

"How long has it been sitting here?" asked Ladderman.

"It was here when I first came. Guilford got it," answered Doc.

"Nobody else probably wanted it," said Clancyman.

"Look, it's ours, an' we kin restore it," countered Tom irritably.

"Right. Wave the magic wand an' look for Tinkerbell," said Clancyman sarcastically.

"You sometimes gets on me nerves," said Tom, his voice rising. Clancyman went back into the staff hut.

"Ow are we gonna move this then?" demanded Dan.

"Grease the axles, then 'tween the wheels an' axles. That'll help when the time comes." Ladderman went back to the tool shed and brought a bucket of grease and did as Tom directed. But the 'Toad' refused to budge. "Not time yet."

Later, when Guilford returned from the bank, he sent Tom to Bonehead Scrappers. About tea time, Tom came back with a tell-tale smile.

Several days later, a standard BR shunter made its cautious way through the connection to Bonehead Scrappers. The engineman's mate leaped off, threw some manual switches, and clambered back on as his mate guided the engine through the points onto a waiting track.

"'Aven't seen them fools 'round 'ere for some time now," commented Chalky as he eased the shunter into the yard.

"Right. No crazy Scotchmen pickin' up trash an' bits o' metal," agreed Sedge.

"Them louts got locked up for awl the trouble they caused," remembered the driver. The engine came to a momentary stop. He lit a cigar, threw his match carelessly out of his side window, and began to chuckle as the shunter lurched forward again.

"Here, mind the matches, you," blurted an overall-clad fellow, wielding a lit blow torch on the driver's side. "Mind 'em yerself!" roared Chalky. Something in his tone, along with his large size, convinced the worker not to argue. He resumed his task while Chalky brought his engine to a complete stop.

"There's the watchman's hut. Go get the papers for that parcels van," ordered Chalky as Sedge made his way to the weather-beaten shack. He knocked on the door, and MacLeish, taking a short break from his rounds, put his tea mug down and opened the door.

"Oy, mate, 'ere t' pick up some old parcels van t' the Scrap an'

Skull," began Sedge. MacLeish handed Sedge the documents and told him the van was on Track #4.

"Well?" enquired Chalky as his mate stood by the cab.

"It's on Track #4."

"We been to this place enough t' know it like our own. Get me through the points."

Once they were out of Bonehead Scrappers and on their way down the line, Chalky looked at his mate and said, "Wot's the name o' the place we're takin' this 'ere van to, anyway? It's got some weird name which I've forgotten. Scrap an'…? Don't recall us ever goin' there before."

"Not that I remember. It's the Scrap and Skull Railway, one o' them enthusiasts' places."

Chalky wasn't sure he had heard right. "The Scrap an' wot?"

"Skull. Used t' be a scrap iron an' metals place. Had their own short line."

"That's beyond all them other fool names I've 'eard. 'The Scrap an' Skull'. Don't that take the cake? Where in the name o' God did they ever get that? An' 'ow d' you know so much about it?"

"Well, Scrap is like the Bone'ead firm. Skull, well, they say one of the founders 'ad an ancestor who was a pirate, or sailed wi' one, or somming akin t' that. An' they used t' paint skulls on the engines but people got superstitious over 'em. So they quit doin' that an' called it the S&S. They 'ad an Open Day there last week. That was in the last *Preserved Railway Review*. You can learn a lot of railway history by readin' that magazine."

"So that's the one you been readin' on our breaks? Well, next time, let me take a look. 'The Scrap an' Skull'. Tomfoolery, pure an' simple."

While Sedge was engaged in enlightening Chalky, they arrived at the connecting track to the S&S. Chalky let go with a few blasts from the engine's horn. Seeing as there was no immediate response from inside the gate, Chalky laid on with an extra long blast. Sedge brightened. A few seconds later, an old gaffer appeared, toddled over to the railway gate (Clancyman wasn't feeling too well today) and wheezed, "Wot d' you want?"

"We got yer van, you bloomin' idiot!" shouted Chalky. "Now let us in."

Clancyman fumbled for the key while Chalky noticed a rusting sign attached to the side of Shed No 6 (nearest one to the permanent way) which had an "S&S" printed in large black letters. The Scrap an' Skull. Looks an' sounds like a graveyard for broken down ol' things an' dead people, he thought to himself. He surveyed the place quietly. When the shunter and its lone consist had cleared the gate, everyone on the property turned out to witness the spectacle of the ex-BR wagon being gently towed into their own yard! Tom took pictures, and Chalky waved while Sedge made his way to the little crowd.

It had been a few years, but Dan and Ladderman recognized Sedge, and fled towards the loo behind the tool shed.

"Hmm. Must be too much tea," thought Tom out loud.

Can you push the van onto the track that leads into that shed, and also get the 'Toad' in there, too?" inquired the Chair hopefully, pointing to Shed No. 2 where the doors had been flung open.

"Both o' them at once?" remarked Clancyman. By this time, Sedge had presented the lading bill (stamped "Paid") to Guilford.

"Sure. But 'e'll 'ave t' back up first." With only a few moves, the shunter was able to push both inside the shed, with Doc signalling from within. Lon secured the hand brake. Sedge climbed back into the cab for the short ride to the fence and BR metals when Chalky had backed out and the switch was thrown. Doc ran up to Chalky's side of the cab.

"Say, how about a cab ride?"

"No. 'Gainst regulations," advised Chalky.

"Come on. One time, for me."

"No." Chalky released the brake and moved the shunter along.

"Let me on. Just this once." Doc, seeing he was not going to get his way, tried to shame the BR crew. "Well, then get yourselves out of here. You remind me of an eyesore." Chalky stopped the engine.

Looking over at Sedge, he said, with some emphasis, "'Eyesore!' Look at who's talkin'! This *place* is an eyesore!"

"We're proud of the Scrap and Skull. A long, proud history! What do you know?"

"I know wot I see." Sedge moved over to his mate's side and leaned out the window. "Called the S&S, it was."

"'The Scrap an' Skull'. Looks more like the 'Sick an' Sad'. That's wot you ought t' call it!" Suddenly, Chalky felt inspired. He began chanting sarcastically:

*"The Sick an' Sad,*
*The Good an' Bad;*
*The Cat an' Dog,*
*The London Fog!"*

Sedge started laughing. Chalky grinned at Sedge and they began together:

*"The Sick an' Sad,*
*The Good an' Bad;*
*The Cat an' Dog,*
*The London Fog!"*

"Any o' those names is as good as the one you've got," finished Chalky after a fit of uncontrollable laughter with his mate. He had gotten in the last word.

"Another bunch o' fools," dismissed Chalky as he took one last look round. "We're on our way." Shaking his head, he released the brake and urged the shunter out the gate, with Sedge throwing the last switch to get them back on BR metals.

Meanwhile, as the Scrap and Skull set were rejoicing over their newly acquired piece of rolling stock, Dan held a quick meeting with Ladderman behind the loo.

"We ain't no nearer t' our goal than when we got 'ere."

"No."

"I say we get the money an' run. Start up our own place."

"But what's left is in the bank. That's stealing, Dan."

"So? We're now members o' this digged down ol' place. We can go in, take it, an' start buyin' Deltic parts."

"Where are we going to keep them? Dan, I've been thinking. Ever since we got here, these chaps have been kind to us."

"Right. Wearin' moth-eaten old clothes from some Salvation place, stayin' in this shack, shavin' inna cold loo, eatin' tinned food an' stale biscuits—"

"Then go back to your manhole!" exploded Ladderman. "I don't know how I ever let you talk me into such a foolhardy scheme. I feel like staying here a while longer, 'til March sometime, helping these fellows make a go of it before I go back to the farm. My brothers don't expect me t' be gone for much longer than that. We talked last week on the telephone."

"Some Deltic man. 'Ave you forgotten yer oath, membership in DOSE?"

"There's more to preservation than trying to salvage bits and pieces of some old engine," dismissed Ladderman. "Ous etes idgiot." He was disgusted with Dan. Time here had been his epiphany. He began walking towards the hut, Dan close behind him.

"Here, wot's this, a secret society?" asked Tom as the rest followed

Ladderman into the hut. “Pass the kettle.”

“No.” Dan was in no mood to be cooperative. He sat down heavily with his cup and glowered at Ladderman.

“Then wot caused you two t’ bolt when BR showed up with our van?”

“Ah... well, can’t swear to it, but… might have been those old scones had mould in them, and made us sick,” offered Ladderman. Clancyman nodded.

“’Appened t’ me last week.”

“We should get some *fresh* ones,” said Dan in anger.

“Suppose you go out and buy them?” asked Lon. No answer.

“Time for another meeting.”

Guilford took up his usual place by the stove as did everyone else. Dan continued glowering.

“Before we proceed, it’s time—” began Ladderman.

“Quiet,” ordered Dan.

“Time… time is ticking, and it waits for no man—”

“How about women? I recall waiting for half an hour when I was seeing ‘Curly’ Anne Sandhill. Pretty girl, with ringlets of hair down her back. Now that girl—” Guilford held his hand up, which nearly ended the beginning of a fond remembrance.

“We’ve got to keep moving. This place is coming along pretty well, but we’ve got so much farther to go. As you know, Ladderman here has drawn up a general plan for the repair and painting of every building on the property except Shed No 6. We need to include it in our plan, or one day, pull it down.”

“I know a little about that sort of thing. Had to take an old building down on a friend’s farm back in Jersey,” remembered Ladderman. “Also I have put up a few sheds and such.” Then: “That girl kept me waiting in her house while she primped for a dance.” Happier times were seen fleeting across his countenance. “La buonne femme.” He sighed with deep regret.

“The question is, do we want to keep it? It’s open for discussion.” But no one advanced a scheme for the shed. Guilford sat down.

Ladderman continued.

"Well, I've been looking at that building. Very strange. Structurally sound, stout wooden beams, large, open floor. It's in better shape than any of the others, with those firm walls, so it's not on the list of urgent repairs. I'm guessing it's the oldest, being nearest the track to the outside. That said, it IS in need of a good scraping and painting. Who put that radio in here?"

"I did," answered Lon.

"Merci. I heard we're getting some unseasonably warm weather next week. I say we decide on a paint scheme, scrape that building's outside walls down, prime it, and paint it before the weather takes our chance away. Roof is surprisingly good."

"'Owd'ya explain that it's in such good shape?" wondered Clancyman.

"Not sure except to put it down to sound building practice. And it was kept up over the years."

"Wait… so wot izzit good for?" pursued Clancyman. "Hain't we got enough buildings 'round 'ere?"

"Well, seeing as it's in good condition… I say we keep it, turn it into something useful. It appears to be one of the first buildings put up. Don't know why it's No 6; it ought to be No 1. We should renumber the buildings."

"Turn it into what?"

"One day, when we find or acquire some artefacts, we could open it up as a museum."

"Excellent! Good thinking, with an eye toward the future. Ladderman, you are a real credit to this group,' said Guilford warmly.

"'E kin be a real minus at times," warned Dan. "'E don't always think 'for 'e talks."

"Around here, Ladderman has definitely become a great asset. He's done a lot, and repaired the sheds, including a few of the roofs. In my opinion, you have been underutilized at your own railway."

"Just getting started," smiled Ladderman.

"Now there's the first grain o' truth I heerd yet," declared Dan slowly.

"Mr Guilford, might I pose a question?" requested Ladderman.

"Certainly. Go on."

"How did you know I was from Jerri?"

"My parents rented a cottage there for a few summers when I was a child. Lovely place. So when you introduced yourself, I recognized the accent."

"Ous avez pale Jerriais?"

"Non."

"Well, I'm happy to learn you enjoyed your time en Jerri."

"I did. Now… shall we proceed on with Shed No 6 as long as weather permits?" A unanimous "Aye" was heard round the hut. Dan put his foot on Ladderman's right toes so as to remind him not to say it twice. "Right. Ladderman, you and Tom will get together and recommend a suitable paint scheme. You will then estimate the amount of primer and paint we'll need. We have plenty of scrapers and brushes in the shed. I'll need the figures tomorrow, and then I'll go get what is necessary." Ladderman and Tom sat near each other and began preliminary discussions. "You can do that a little later, please." He paused. "Remember at one time we were exploring the purchase of a small engine—"

"Oh, no, not that stick burner," groaned Clancyman.

"Stick burner?" chimed in Dan and Ladderman together, looking at each other.

Ladderman's mind turned to the shunter he had seen earlier that day. "Say, what about that shunter that brought in the parcels van? Be just the right size."

"That crew uses it for light work. I know the driver must use a larger engine for his other shifts," informed Tom.

"The 'Fancy Stair'—"

"What is the 'Fancy Stair'?"

"Nothing but a stick burner an' waste o' time," complained Clancyman.

"An engine that burns sticks? The times call for something more practical," suggested Ladderman, shaking his head.

"How much will that tank cost?" asked Doc, having forgotten the details.

"You will remember that is was a sealed tender affair," reminded Guilford. "We have entertained other options, but this is the one we need to have closure on. I have contacted our benefactor, who has given us a provisional nod." He produced an envelope with the same information. "But something must be done first."

"So this outfit has decided on a steam engine, then? Wot about Dai Woodhams'?" Dan had seen articles concerning the engines being sold to enthusiast groups for restoration.

"Tom is the only one who could help restore one. But we don't have the tools or the parts. It would be frightfully expensive, more than the 'Fancy Stair'."

"I see."

"Here, 'ow do we know if it's worth a tender?" persisted Clancyman.

"Precisely. That is what we need Dan for." All eyes were fixed on him, but blank stares revealed the want of purpose. "Dan, we need you to go inspect the 'Fancy Stair' for us. None of us is qualified except Tom, and he has some family business this coming week. Will you do it?"

Dan quickly considered. Perhaps this was one way to commend himself to the others. He felt his hold on Ladderman slipping away fast, if it still existed at all. He had discarded Dan's 'Scrap and Skull Scheme' for the present endeavour. How would he get his Deltic rebuilt under these circumstances? Probably not here. Time for alternate plans.

"Yes, I'll go, wherever it is."

"The Snakepit and Froggy Pond Railway, located 20 miles from Birmingham, up in your part of the world. Come to think of it, it has been closed for a few years, at least. An enthusiast group couldn't make a go of it. Anyway, it's near a BR station called Deer Pond." Guilford spoke in hopeful terms. Others groaned, sighed or voiced strong objections. Guilford thought there was a chance the engine could be obtained for a reasonable sum. He tried to convince his friends that it was a viable possibility. Of course, the engine would need a careful inspection first….

"Well, Dan, that be not far from you." Tom lit his pipe. Dan refused to allow this line of thought.

"Here, not so much smoke," snapped Dan. "There be enough bad air that we 'ave t' breathe." Tom politely knocked the tobacco out of his pipe.

"There should be a 'No Smoking' rule in 'ere. This is where we meet, 'ave our breaks, and live," persisted Dan, looking at his friend. "Can't open no windows this time o' year." Guilford nodded and the new rule was adopted.

"Take lots of pictures and plenty of detailed notes. Here is a writing tablet and pen. Take down all the specifics. Tom will want to go over them with you. And here's enough to tide you over for the day," as he thrust some banknotes into Dan's greasy hand. Dan secretly laughed to himself, glad that he wouldn't have to use anything from his private stash of bills he had hoarded since first arriving from his trip down. Dan smiled and thanked the Chair.

The ride to Deer Pond was fairly uneventful save for Dan nicking two wallets that somehow fell out of their owners' pockets. The contents removed, the wallets were placed on alternative carriage seats and found by other riders, who courted deep suspicion. He netted 250 pounds for his troubles.

As soon as the train stopped at the station, he alighted, spotted a Wimpy Bar, knew it was time to eat, went round the back, and opened the door. Five workers were in a frenzy, tying to keep up with the lunch crowd. Dan hid his camera and tablet under a nearby bush, strolled in, washed his hands, flung on an apron and a Wimpy hat which he found on a peg near the door, and proceeded to fry burgers. The chap whose permanent job it was to serve up the steaming beef had taken ill that very morning.

“Hello, you don’t look familiar,” a pimply-faced stripling commented as he pulled chips out of the boiling grease.

“That’s because I jus’ got ’ired yesterday, Junior,” grinned Dan as the first lot came off the stove.

“Get a bath, will you?”

“You the new man Sonnie hired yesterday?” demanded the day manager as he came nearer to the oven.

“That be me,” answered Dan, putting some new patties on the hot surface.

“Don’t recall seeing you on my roster. What’s your name?”

Pause. Then, “Nick… Nick Ring.”

“Right, Nick. Well, you seem to know what you’re doing.” Penter walked away and began assisting with orders. “Keep the burgers coming, Nick.”

Customers began commenting on how well the burgers were prepared, “Not overdone an’ dry, but moist an’ tasty.” Nick heard these pronouncements and grinned to himself. It wasn’t bad work; in fact, it was rather pleasant. More orders kept coming and some were from the same customers.

About three hours later Nick finished frying the last of the lunch orders, made four burgers for himself, squirted mustard on them, wrapped them in paper, and wiped his area down to a shine. He even cleaned the stove top surface. Then, when no one was looking, he stuck his apron and Wimpy hat on the same peg where he had found them, slid out the back door, grabbed the camera and tablet, and fled. Sitting behind a parked car, he wolfed down his lunch. “Mmm. Coulda used more mustard.”

Faded signs pointed him in the direction of the Snakepit and Froggy Pond Railway as Dan made his way to the boarded-up station of Snakepit. Several fruitless searches up and down the weed-choked, deserted platform led Dan to conclude that the moribund operation was about to give him an excuse to leave for greener pastures. Behind a derelict shed, a slight old man approached him slowly, and with interest.

"Yesh?"

"I'm Diesel – I'm from the Scrap Skull Railway, 'ere t' inspect the engine you 'ave put up for sale. My letter of introduction and our tender." He handed the letter and sealed tender to the old man. Armsby began to read Dan's letter, written by Guilford. "Where is this thing?" Dan brandished a camera and tablet.

"After me." Armsby bent an already crooked finger at Dan, motioning him to follow along an overgrown dirt path to another boarded-up building. Paint peeled from the sides, the roof sagged, one wall appeared to lean, two tiny windows had no glass in them, but the large wooden doors were stout and strong. "In 'ere." Dan threw open the doors and beheld the sight before him. The 'Fancy Stair' had not been steamed for a few years. Several cobwebs hung across the footplate. The air smelled like something had recently died.

"Another dead rat? Bill! Come over 'ere. Tell thish Inspector 'bout the engine." Bill entered the dank confines from an unknown location. He was short, bald, and bespectacled. He began lecturing Dan by saying: "Mr lckthee and Mr Ackthee were not only friends, but very distant neighbours."

"Who? Are those *real* names? 'Ow distant?"

"One day Mr Ickthee, who lived near Deer Pond, decided to visit Mr Ackthee, who lived near Froggy Pond. They decided that the best way to visit was to build a railway of their very own."

"Didn't they think o' ridin' 'orses or somming? Walkin'? Hmm. A private line," said Dan quietly.

"Very good, Herman. So they did. After the nine-mile stretch was built back in 1860, they bought a single carriage and began casting about for a proper engine."

"They wasn't distant neighbours. They wasn't 'neighbours' at all. So they got this?"

"Very good, Herman," declared Bill.

"Me name's not 'erman."

"I KNOW who you are."

"Oh, yeah? An' 'ow iz that?"

"So they engaged the Stick and Coal Fire Loco Company to build them an engine."

"A stick burner! Why didn't they get a coal-burning engine?"

"After the first journey was completed to Deer Pond, the two men enjoyed a hearty bowl of longstew."

"Is it good?"

"Very. It's a local speciality. You can have some at Agnes's, a block from the BR station." Dan was looking round, trying to listen to this nonsense, and keep a straight face.

"I thought this line was called the Bird Pigeon Pit or such," said Dan dismissively.

"Herman, very, very bad," complained Bill, wagging his finger at Dan.

"I'm NOT 'erman!" yelled Dan. His voice filled the cavernous old shed, then died away.

"After Mr lckthee died around 1903, Mr Ackthee passed away, in 1904. A snake pit was found near Deer Pond, as Mr Ickthee was wont to tell anyone who would listen while he was alive, and was cleansed of the reptiles. Maybe that is why so many dogs had succumbed to death in Deer Pond. Poultry farmers moved into the area and bought the line. Other industries located along the line as well. Their problem was the 'Fancy Stair', since it had been designed to pull one or two carriages at most, and couldn't cope with the increased tonnage of goods vans loaded for the connection to the Midland."

"But poultry don't weigh that much."

"Herman, you just don't know, do you? The line stayed in use until the 1960s."

"Then wot?"

"The engine was used for excursion purposes now and then for the enthusiasts who tried to make a go of the line, but after 1980, that ended."

"So wot was used for regular power? Any Deltics on the line?"

"We're trying to locate the 'Fancy Stair's' replacement. We think it may have been an Adams 02 or similar type. A tank engine. No

Deltics. Now, Inspector Herman, proceed."

Dan's middle name *was* Herman, but this was not general knowledge. Who was this Bill, anyway? He felt nettled, but tried to let it pass. He knew show time was on.

"Axlesh, running gear, 'ave all been kept lubricated an' greashed," mouthed Armsby. "Shomebody needsh tah take care of it. I'm getting old."

Dan took out Guilford's camera and began taking pictures of the 'Fancy Stair'. It was a light 0–4–0, but Dan did not even know that. He ascended the footplate and brushed the webs aside. He slid under the frame and tried to think of what to photograph, and ended up taking too many pictures of the stairs, and forgot or didn't know to take shots of the valve gear, smokebox, tank and bunker, driver's and firemen's sides in the cab, firebox, etc. Then he put the camera down and pretended to scribble notes to himself, all the while drawing cartoonish caricatures of Armsby and Bill. Armsby watched him critically. Having no knowledge of steam power, he groped for ideas, but his usual flair failed him miserably. He deliberately spent at least 5 minutes on the side of the engine where they could not see him.

"Leave him to it," Armsby mumbled as he and Bill filed out.

Dan sat down nearest the left front wheel. What would be his next move? What would he tell them back at the S&S? Later he emerged from the shed, trying to look as serious as he could, after listening to that ridiculous story about 'Ickthee and Ackthee'. Armsby stood by the boarded-up station.

"Sho? What do you think?"

"I'll… 'ave t' submit me report t' the Society. Then we will make a decision."

"Right."

"'Ow many offers 'ave been tendered?"

"I'm not at liberty to shay."

"Tell me."

"Itsh a shealed tender. Be on your way, Shkipper."

"Skipper?"

"Yesh. Shkip on out of here."

"Then watch me go, Rickety!" yelled Dan and he skipped past the boarded-up station, through a car park, and onto the sidewalk which would take him to Deer Pond Station. He crossed the street entering Agnes's, about one block from the station. "Bowl of longstew." True to Bald-Headed Bill's prediction, Dan admired the taste greatly as he ate. He washed it down with Newcastle Ale. After leaving a crumpled bill as payment, he went outside and walked behind the Wimpy Bar and considered his 'Nick Ring' debut. Should he try it again? What's the worst that could happen? Being tossed out of a Wimpy Bar did not leave him trembling in fear.

So he took a deep breath, jammed the hat in place, and began cutting lettuce.

"Here, that's my job. Gimme that lettuce," whined another pimply-faced stripling.

"Well, it's my job now," answered Dan, pushing him away. "Go fetch me some more."

Mr Penter came over to the counter where the salads were prepared. "Nick! Where have you been?"

"I took me break."

"Break? You get one when I *tell* you! We really needed you. All of a sudden we got a large crowd off some 'bus. Don't ever leave us like that again. Now hand that knife over to Sammy. Get back over to the stove...."

"Mind if I bring me camera in 'ere?"

"What for?"

"Me mum's idea. Seems I'm the first one off the dole in three generations."

"Well, I think that's great. But take pictures later. We've got orders." Indeed, hungry customers were already waiting. So Nick was busy for hours. Again, customers commented on the 'great taste', which Penter gladly accepted with a nod to his new employee. Nick had been adding a few extra shakes of something he found in the back room. Why hadn't they been doing this before? Was it some secret spice he had stumbled onto? He did not overcook the burgers either, which added to the compliments as before. Duplicate and return orders for the second time were being received. The cash register was kept busier than usual, and Penter was silently grateful for the upturn in business. It would look good on the weekly report!

Nick realized that he'd miss his connections if he stayed much longer. But Penter asked him to fill in for a while as the evening cook had been delayed by a family emergency. So he remained until business slacked off. The cook still had not shown up, but he had to leave. He hastily made four burgers, squirted mustard on them (but not enough), jammed two fistfuls of chips in his greasy pockets, placed his apron and hat on the peg by the backdoor, and slid out the door. He grabbed the Society's camera and tablet and ran to Deer Pond Station. He was buying his tickets as the train warned of its approach. Few moments were those in Dan's life when things happened to work so well.

Once Dan found a seat, he made short work of the chips. Chomping down on the first burger, Dan realized he had forgotten extra mustard again. A loud curse emanated from bits of seared beef, cheese, wilted lettuce, and partly crushed bun.

"That's no way to talk," scolded a grandmotherly type with a little pinched-faced boy.

"Shut yer mouth, Granny," said Dan with a sneer.

"You rude man. Don't talk to me Grandmum like that," added the little boy, his face even more pinched. Dan noticed he had a ski-jump-like nose. He tore off a small piece of the sandwich, reached across the aisle, ski-jumped the piece off his nose, and shoved it into the boy's mouth.

"That'll shut you up, Junior."

True to his prediction, 'Junior' forgot all about the harsh language directed against his grandmother, and consumed the food in an instant.

"I want more."

"No."

"I want more."

"Well, you can't 'ave any more."

Junior went into a tantrum. "More more more!"

A quick slap caused Junior to howl terribly. His cries drew the attention of the entire carriage. Grandmum tried to console Junior, but to no avail. A large man, who had witnessed the entire incident, made his way to Dan's seat. Dan, however, kept eating. A sudden jolt from a quick application of the brakes caused him to fall to the floor with a loud thud. He tried to get up slowly to face Dan as the carriage rocked back and forth.

"Where d' you get away wi' smackin' little tykes?"

Dan didn't answer. Instead, he seized two spent fags from the floor, stood up, stuck them in the man's large ears, and exclaimed, "Here, look at the bloke from Mars! I always thought you fellows was *green*." Squeals of laughter broke out from every seat in the fully occupied carriage, and even Junior stopped crying, looked at the 'man from Mars', and laughed, slapping his hands on his legs. The large man now had a red face in addition to his recently acquired 'equipment'.

"Say, that's a good trick, changing colours like that," continued Dan. "Tell us, 'ow d'you do it?"

"Like this!" A sudden blow from a burly right fist caught Dan unawares as he was sent sprawling back into his seat. The large man, now labelled 'Martian' by the passengers, still angry, forgot about his 'antennae' as he returned to his seat. No one wanted to spoil the fun, and Dan, nursing a swelling cheek, did not pursue any further, finished his dinner in silence (chewing on the left). The Martian ended up going home wondering why people were laughing at him at every turn of the side- walk. Dan's ride to London was uneventful.

He had stayed too long at the Wimpy Bar, and missed his previously planned connecting train to Factory Furnace. That meant the last one on the line that night, and he missed the gate closing at the S&S as well. Ladderman, being in essence locked in, could not offer any assistance, so he could not enter the premises until morning, when Clancyman returned. He trudged back to the station to spend the night. Chased out by a stolid member of the police, he wandered aimlessly round until he found shelter from the cold wind in back of an old brick-walled warehouse. Its arched windows reminded him of a similar building he once saw in Wales, but a fitful sleep hunched in between two dustbins deprived him of further recollection.

Dan awoke with a start. He could have sworn he heard bagpipe music. No, not that dream again! He looked round to make sure. No one was there.... The sun had only been up a while and he shivered in the cold. He reasoned it was past eight. Slowly, painfully, he rose to his feet, slung the camera over his shoulder, and trudged off to the Scrap and Skull Railway. Later he found his co-workers huddled round the stove and gave Ladderman a hard shove.

"What's that for, eh?"

"Could 'ave let me in last night if Clancyman 'ere'd give you a key."

"You're vexed with the wrong person."

"So where'd you sleep?" asked the old gate keeper.

"Spent the night inna fouull place." He warmed himself by the heating stove.

"Yeah. That accounts for your *smell*," commented Lon. "How about a good scrubbing in the shower?"

"In the cold!" yelled Dan. "It ain't hot water, you know!"

"I take one every day. Got used to it," said Ladderman. "Once you get used to it—"

"Shut up!" yelled Dan again. "I 'ad t' sleep 'tween two dustbins."

"Well, those dustbins. That sounds familiar. Reminds me of the time we got thrown out of the Madd Dogg Inn...." Another elbow precisely aimed cut off any further discourse on the subject.

"'Ow did ya get that lump?" Clancyman pointed to Dan's right cheek.

"Slipped an' fell inna Wimpy Bar. 'Ad me dinner there." Dan produced some greasy Wimpy wrappers and a few soggy chips, which disappeared.

"Where's yer notes? Wot did you find out?"

"Thought you 'ad family business in Kent."

"Done. Came back sooner than I expected. May 'ave t' go back, though. Or up t' Essex."

A chill suddenly went through Dan's overly ripe body. Tom was a steam man, and he could not fake it.

"So… where's yer notes?"

Pause. "They was stole. I laid 'em down and some bloke named 'erman took 'em." He produced a few pieces of paper from the tablet, but they had Armby's and Bill's caricatures on them. "That fellow likes t' draw. He stoled my notes, but left these." Tom took the papers and passed them around. Ladderman thought they were funny, but the rest did not laugh. Yet.

"Who are these chaps, eh?"

"That's some old flintlock and Bald-'eaded Bill." Then Dan told the Ickthee/Ackthee story, which made Clancyman roll off his chair, holding his sides. Even Tom could not keep from smiling.

"A bad jape, at best."

"Surely that fellow was up some wrong alley, or went t' the pub early?"

"How does Herman know so much about the place?"

"'E told it with a straight face. Must be true, but sounds outlandish t' me."

"Why would some bloke named 'erman steal yer notes, an' leave you these silly drawings?" Silence. "Then give me the camera. I'll take the film t' be developed." Dan handed the camera to Tom.

"I want t' know why them notes was stolen," declared Clancyman, recovering after his fit of laughter on the floor.

"I already said, some bloke named 'erman took 'em."

"Herman? Herman who?" wondered Guilford.

"Don't know that one. 'E had come from the… Bird Pigeon Pit or some such place t' inspect the engine, like me. Must've 'ad a tender on it. I laid me tablet down t' take pictures an' he jus must've took

’em, leaving the tablet an’ these drawings. ’E left before I could chase after ’im.” Dan stopped, unsure of where he would go from there. He was unwittingly helped by the volunteers. They bombarded him with questions. Dan did his best, and then held up a hand for silence, as Guilford did when a meeting was coming to order. After taking a deep breath, he glibly stated that: “The pictures will show everything I said. In my opinion… it’s unwise for us t’ try an’ get the ‘Fancy Stair’, because it’s not suitable.” Dan settled back in his chair with an air of cautious triumph. But it was not over.

“Unsuitable? How so?” asked Doc.

“I could… cite technicals, but I’ll spare you. To… put it simply… the engine needs a great deal o’ work, beyond anything we can do ’ere. The cost would be too ’igh.” He attempted a grave face.

“Wot would the cost be?”

Dan panicked. He thought *that* would have been enough. He remembered the last time he was on the spot and tried to be smart, so he stated rather flatly, “Upwards of a five-figured sum.”

“A five-figured sum!” shouted everyone else. Doc shook his head slowly.

“A stick burner,” scolded Clancyman. “An’ yer an educated man.”

“Wot’s this Railway want with a stick burner, eh?” queried Ladderman. “Put it out of your head. As I said before, the times call for something practical. Like that shunter we saw in here.”

“Truly spoken,” agreed Guilford. “Well, gentlemen, are we all in union to put the matter to rest?”

“Nil. Not ’til we’ve seen the pictures,” argued Tom.

“Then it’s tabled until we’ve had a chance to examine them.”

Dan spent a fitful night, haunted by the ‘flintlock’, mouthing something he could not understand.

A few days later, when all the chores were done for the day, someone noticed Tom was not on site. He had shown up that day, but where had he gone? After a few steaming cups of tea, Clancyman went round the property but could not locate him. Calls to his family in Kent did not prove helpful but his brother did mention he had some cousins in Essex he hadn't seen for a few years. He could not pass along the telephone number in Essex, or was unwilling to. That night the talk centred around Tom and Dan's pictures. Everyone admired the look of the 'Fancy Stair', but no one made positive comments on the lack of the technical close-ups needed for final approval. Dan sat somewhat away from the rest, drinking extra cups of tea to hide his silence. Since neither subject proved fruitful, the little group broke up around seven, leaving Ladderman and Dan to the hut, and their own speculation.

The next two weeks brought more changes. Dan grew further resentful and chafed under Ladderman's growing authority. Guilford and the group planned for more Open Days. A warm front had ushered in some unusually temperate weather and that convinced Ladderman to take advantage of it by ordering the final scraping and preparation of Shed No 6. Why this move? Ladderman had determined that, once all the sheds had been repaired, scraping, priming, and painting should begin (weather permitting), starting with the shed having the highest number, and then working backwards. It did not hurt that Shed No 6 was in the best condition, and that could have influenced him. No 6 happened to be the one closest to BR metals, but that did not predispose his judgment. He had already noted its sound construction and condition. He had performed some minor repairs on it already. Also, he wanted the men to taste success, and No 6 would not prove to be a great obstacle to that goal. A smartly turned-out building would certainly boost morale.

Tom and Ladderman had agreed that the colours should fit the era and use of the building. They had selected dark grey lined with black, in deference to its age. Under close supervision, the volunteers save Tom set to task quickly, completing the task of scraping and priming the entire building in several days, with minimal breaks. In the midst of a near derelict scrap yard, Shed No 6 began to look like a miracle. Ladderman insisted on putting two coats of paint, allowing it to thoroughly dry each time. Thus they were employed for more than a week. New hinges and locks were added as well. The weather was cooperating a few days beyond its forecasted welcome, but they knew that to expect more was not realistic. Guilford took pictures and sent them off for enlarging. They were to grace the staff hut's walls. A smartly turned-out building indeed!

The colour scheme looked so good on the shed that it was decided to complete the other ones using the authentic-looking dark grey lined with black. But then the weather shifted to its usual stance, and further preparation was called off. Ladderman was grateful that he had planned enough time for the paint to dry before winter had returned. It was already March, and spring was not too distant. But there was no let-up in winter's tight grasp this time. So back they went to cleaning out the sheds, hauling trash to the dustbins, some inside repair work, and planned for more. Dan hated the tasks at hand and fantasized about running away to Deer Pond, working at the Wimpy Bar, and eating all the burgers and chips he could stuff into his mouth. The latest Deltic scheme began to fade with each burger he craved. And so the days passed.

One cold winter morning, Ladderman was directing and assisting in the repair of a wall in Shed No 5 when a shrill whistle startled everyone. Guilford held up a hand as a sign for them to stop. The sound repeated itself as well as the flat blaring of a diesel horn. Guilford motioned his group to walk in the direction of the railway gate. The urgent sounds caused a collective quickening of paces, but Dan's curiosity caused him to outrun them all. When he arrived at the gate, he beheld a sight which left him speechless. A standard shunter had stopped at the battered railway gate, and behind it was the 'Fancy Stair', under its own steam, with Tom on the footplate! A feeble arm gripped the left side of the engine cab. Dan watched a very slow-moving form stand by Tom. It was that ancient, Armsby! He peered at Dan, then began raising his voice at him, waving an arthritic arm while trying to shout something inaudible above the escaping steam.

The shunter's driver, impatient at the apparent lack of response from the Scrap and Skull, alighted from his cab to encourage Dan, or someone else, to open the padlocked gate. However, should the reader wish to enquire, the BR driver crew were not our intrepid friends, Chalky and Sedge, who had booked on to other goods duties. The BR driver did possess something of Chalky's outlook as he demanded some force of action be taken.

"Here! Get this gate open! I hain't got all the live long day!"

"'Aven't got the key," was his answer in monotone. Dan couldn't manage much else. Armsby was still trying to show his anger.

"Then get one! I hain't got time t' while away."

Guilford and Clancyman brushed past Dan with the olden set of necessary keys. As the railway gate was thrown open, screeching as it cleared the track, a switch was thrown, Tom pulled the whistle chord with glee, the driver got back into his cab, and both locos seemed to glide by, with the 'Fancy Stair' hissing loudly. Everyone present stood in awe: Guilford recovered to signal that the engine should be put on Track 1.

Ladderman had hoped and planned that one day Shed No 1 would be used to actually store or keep an engine. But he did not think it would be needed so soon! He made mental calculations for the work needed to be done inside. Luckily, the shed had been emptied of rubbish, and the track area inside was cleared. He had repaired the skylight in the roof, and noted that it could be opened or closed. He determined it was in working order. But to think they would use it today!

Tom uncoupled the engine from the shunter. It pulled ahead of the 'Fancy Stair'. Doc threw a switch while Clancyman unlocked the doors to Shed No 1. Armsby eased the engine into the shed, smiling like the Cheshire Cat. Ladderman pulled on a long lever and the glass sides of the skylight sprang open. He left the doors open to air out the place and to welcome its new inhabitant! With little ceremony, Doc helped the BR crew through the points back unto the permanent way, but not before a sheaf of documents was handed to Guilford, who clutched them to his chest with great emotion. Dan still stood by the gate, dumbfounded. His already addled mind had not yet begun to wrap itself round the recent events.

Clancyman had walked back to the railway gate and then returned to admire the engine. He noticed that there was coal in the bunker, not cut wood, or sticks for that matter.

Tom stepped off the footplate while Armsby remained. Guilford was the first to speak.

"Tom! Where have you been? We tried to locate your whereabouts. Did you go to Essex?"

"At ease, lads. After your imposter 'Dan' came back with that strange story, I went t' see for myself. That bloke don't know Armsby 'n' me are old friends, mates on the Southern. That's right! He kept this engine in fine fettle, didn't you?" A quick nod was his answer. He was polishing handles and gauges. "Come down from there! Intr'duce yerself t' the men!" Armsby turned from the gauges with what looked like tears.

"I wanted t' shee her run again, I did. Onesh a shteam man, alwaysh. Pleash, allow me—"

"All right, old friend! Steady on!"

Guilford now spoke with something between surprise and elation. "Now, Tom, please honour us with an explanation! Is this on loan to us, or what?"

"Well, all good news! It's been taken very good care of, steamed occasionally, and run as well. Still on its boiler certificate."

By this time Dan had wandered over to the shed and stared at the engine dully.

"Dan said it wouldn't run. It would cost too much to fix it," reminded Lon.

"Did anyone else bid on it? What about the sticks, eh?"

"'Ow did you get the engine? We didn't ever 'ear 'bout the outcome."

"Well, Armsby knew that I 'ad been party to this society, an' he gave us the inside track, if you don't mind the pun. He set aside our letter for serious consideration. The next day he rang me up an' told me t' come up there once 'Dan' had left. So I went up t' inspect it myself, since 'Dan' told us a tale. I made some calls to BR myself, and put it a few good words for our Railway."

"What about the expenses?"

"All taken care of. Seems the fellows at BR up that way know our benefactor. I 'ad no contact with 'im, but they did. He arranged for the purchase and also the cost of the move!" Shouts of approval rang out like gunshots. Not even Guilford had any idea or hope of the tidings. "Whoever that man is, 'e moves in very 'igh circles," finished Tom.

"Circles an' puns be damned!" yelled Dan as he advanced towards the men with a raised shovel. Doc quickly turned, and, with a deliberate move, spun him round in an instant, causing him to fall down heavily, while Lon grabbed the shovel. Armsby, observing the whole but brief escapade from the footplate, grinned momentarily. Afterwards, he leaned out the right side, and said, "Sherves 'im right!" Tom and the rest glared at Dan with what looked like something akin to hatred.

"You confounded liar! You call yerself a loco inspector! Well, the game's over. When you came back from Birmingham, I knew something was wrong. You claimed you 'ad yer notes stole by some bloke named 'erman, an' yer pictures was no good at all. And while I was up there I did some checkin' on you. There *is* no 'Kickcloth an' Seamside Railway!'" said Tom accusingly. A collective gasp was heard. "Armsby told me about you as well. He realized you wasn't a steam man soon after you walked into that shed." Another collective gasp was heard (except from Ladderman, who had remained silent the first time).

"'Ow perceptive of him," replied Dan sarcastically, rubbing his head with his dirty right hand, still on the shed floor.

"What about the sticks, eh?" repeated Ladderman. Clancyman gave him a shove and then pointed to the bunker.

"If this idiot Dan had bothered t' ask or even *look*, the loco always burned coal, right, Armsby?" A quick nod was his answer.

"But the article said it was a stick burner," said Ladderman. "I read it over myself."

"It did not. It said the loco was built by a firm and the name had

'Stick' in it. That's where we went wrong," corrected Lon.

"Well, we have a water column. I managed to t' get it t' work again. The connections were never cut off. Works pretty well. Had to prime it," reflected Ladderman. "Now we're going to need it."

"I been meanin' to ask this for months: 'ow d' ya know t' be so 'andy, Jacob?" asked Clancyman.

"On a farm, you have to know how to fix things. No time or money to call in someone. Chein qu j'ai' te a faithe."

"Get to the telephone. We need to order some coal. Make an assessment of the bunker's capacities, Tom," directed Guilford. He wrote a few figures down on a small piece of paper. As he made his way to the staff hut, Armsby pointed an arthritic finger at Dan.

"Thish man ish an imposter. Time t' leave, Shkipper."

"'Skipper?' There you go, callin' me names again!" Dan got to his feet, but it was too late. Lon, Guilford, and Doc grabbed him by all fours and carried him to the gate, and after it was unlocked, threw Dan into the street. He rolled over a few times, ending up in the gutter. "Be gone and *never* come back!" yelled Doc. Dan was pelted with pebbles and stones until he got up and ran away from the hostile scene. Ladderman was too stunned to move. He watched Armsby on the footplate, and thought about how far removed he was from the schemes and machinations of DOSE, one member in particular.

In an ironic twist of fate, Ladderman was never questioned about his involvement with the 'Kickcloth and Seamside', and once mid-March had arrived, was obliged to return to his dairy farm in Jersey. In subsequent years, he would spend a few months at the Scrap and Skull, superintending the building and maintenance work, planning future projects, and timetables for completion. His sympathetic brothers allowed this as his reward for hard work and due diligence. Ladderman was basically a decent, hard-working fellow, but his former gullibility had led him astray on highly questionable missions. He had resolved that since he had landed in good company quite by accident, he would devote any time off to the present endeavour. Not so Dan, whose truly hare-brained schemes had done him great harm again and again. Now, banished for the Scrap and Skull, he was back on the lam, completely on his own, with nothing but his own addled wits.

The situation in which Dan found himself was all too familiar: no friends, no gainful means of employment, and nowhere to live. Going back to Pudding Lane was not an option. The hour was almost nine, and the day held the promise of at least some attempt at enterprise. A flickering idea suddenly appeared as he trudged aimlessly down Factory Furnace Road: an image of a figure bent over a hot oven… the kitchen of delight… the re-emergence of 'Nick'.

But before 'Nick' could make his reappearance, he had to live up to his name.

Remembering the whereabouts of the Salvation Army's local branch, Dan wheeled himself round, crossed the nearly empty street, and headed towards the former scene of charity by Guilford. Stepping into the street, he smeared dirt and grease from the gutter onto the right side of his face. This slovenly-looking effect worked perfectly. Shuffling into the place, Dan cast his eyes about blankly, not focusing on any particular object.

"Wot kin I help you with, friend?" asked a kindly older man with a big stomach and an easy smile. Dan lowered his head and his gaze, and, in a muffled voice, whispered, "Spent th' night inna fouull gutter."

Mr Smiley began frowning. "Well, now, we can't have that, my friend. Look at that soiled coat of yours. Let's get a new one." Mr Smiley led Dan to a surplus clothing room. He selected a long black one, and handed it to Dan, who flung off his old one of too many months of constant wear. It was placed in a dustbin which occupied the far corner. On the way out, he tucked another one under the black coat as Mr Smiley led the way. 'Nick' was back.

Fifteen minutes later, Nick was hawking the shorter coat five corners away.

"Wouldn't let a *dog* sleep in it," said the first passerby.

"Twenty pound? Hahaha," scoffed the second. Seeing the futility, Nick hit upon another approach.

"Oh, oh, me poor Nuncle," he wailed, assuming an imaginary air of bereavement. "Oh, me Nuncle," Nick cried as he dabbed his eyes and sniffed.

"Eh?" A matronly woman with iron grey hair walked up to him.

"Oh, Missus, Me Nuncle Ned, an accident, oh, a long death, an' only 'is coat left! An' I mus' sell it as it took all money t' burry 'im." More sniffles followed.

"There, there, poor man," offered Mrs Iron Grey. "It's going t' be awl right. Let me see this coat." She held it out and gave it a long glance. Then she gave a start. Looking quickly inside, she handed it back roughly.

"Wot wuz 'is name?"

"Oh, Missus, it was Ned… Ned Clancyman."

"Ned Clancyman! When did he die?"

"Las' week. The funeral wuz at the… Ebe Wibbitt Memory Chapel."

Mrs Iron Grey held up her right hand. "Stop yer lyin'. Do you know who Samuel Notchkey was?"

Nick stopped 'crying' and dried some invisible 'tears'.

"Who?"

"Me 'usband! I given this coat to the Salvation Army after 'e passed away not two weeks ago! Look! There's 'is name, sewed under the collar!"

Nick dropped the coat and sped off down a nearby alley.

That night, Nick stuck to nicking questionable items from dustbins, especially the one behind the 'Egg Foo Yung Garden'. Later, Nick seized upon the chance to pilfer the pockets of some fellow nickers sleeping in a dark alley. He spent a fitful night behind a deserted building. Bagpipe music gave him more nightmares.

The next day, cold and hungry, Dan hatched another hare-brained scheme: he knew life would be nearly untenable in this area, so, as a final gesture, he would say his goodbyes to Bonehead Scrappers.

Dan scurried down Factory Furnace Road to the scrap yard, where he found the gates chained and padlocked as before. MacLeish was not expecting anyone so early, so he saw no reason why the gates should be open. A quick check told him that the railway gate was locked as well. Dan ran up to the gate breathlessly anyway. Observing the means of security, he reasoned (?) that he could overcome them. He tried to scale the fence, but his Salvation Army coat became entangled in the barbed wire. Dan managed to wriggle out of it, and fell to the gravel surface. All the sound of the chains and lock banging against the gate roused MacLeish's attention. He walked over to the gate as Dan flew round the corner and hid behind the same brick-walled warehouse.

MacLeish noticed the coat, checked the locks, and pulled on the coat. Tug as he might, he could not remove it. Turning round, he saw no living soul, and then, in a twinkling of an eye, set Dan's coat afire with a pocket lighter. Dan stood up and watched his coat go up in flames. MacLeish strolled back to his hut, chuckling to himself. "That'll teach whomever t' think twice before he tries that again."

Little did he know Dan had just made other plans. Gone were the fond thoughts of yesterday's noble goals. Gone were the grand schemes of resurrecting the Deltic from the ashes of sure destruction. Gone were the 'MSC', 'Scotch Kilt', 'Save from Inchey's', and 'Scrap and Skull' schemes.

MacLeish had burned his only means of keeping warm. Revenge dominated his misdirected, addled mind. Dan slammed himself into the road gates, trying to shake them violently. Then he ran behind the warehouse and crouched. MacLeish came out of his hut, inspected the padlock and chains, looked to his left and right, then returned inside. Dan repeated this cat-and-mouse game several times, hoping to draw MacLeish out of the yard.

The fourth time proved decisive. MacLeish, clearly impatient and vexed, unlocked the gates and looked down the west side of the road. Dashing in behind the old Scot, Dan ran over to the shed, found an old newspaper, but searched vainly for matches. His new plan of burning down the watchman's hut as an act of revenge lacked one essential element. Grasping at any idea, Dan tried to rip the door off its hinges, but found it well secured. He tried leaning against the hut, throwing rocks at the thick windows, etc. but nothing was going right. Finally he gave up and left in utter dejection, with some help from MacLeish, who gave him a very convincing shove, followed by a swift kick which sent him sprawling. The chains and padlock resumed their former positions.

The 10:11 pulling into Deer Pond was three minutes late. A cold wind was blowing an errant newspaper round the platform as Dan jumped off the carriage. Weeks of no bath and filthy clothing had given him the back half of the carriage to himself.

Weakened from days of little sustenance, Dan wandered aimlessly until he found a quiet corner in a back alley. There he dozed until the next morning. He got up, dusted himself off, wandered back to the Wimpy Bar, waited 'til eleven when 'his' shift began, opened the back door cautiously, observed the usual confusion, washed his face and hands, spotted 'his' apron and Wimpy hat on the back wall peg, flung on the apron, jammed the hat on his greasy head, strode over to the oven, and began frying patties. Penter, seeing a figure bending over the oven, grabbed the scruffy neck, turned him round, and tried to recognize his employee.

"Who the devil are you?"

"It's me, Guv, Nick. 'Ow are ya?"

"Nick! Where the #!@ have you been?"

"Me Nuncle died. Ned Clancyman. Died in Belfast."

"Ireland!"

"Right. 'ad t' see 'bout me Mum." Nick turned the patties over.

"You're fired. Filthy beggar of a man."

"Fired?"

"You left without notice. Left us in the lurch, you did. We've got no place for your ilk."

Nick threw down his spatula and headed towards the back door. He grabbed two burgers and put them into his pockets. He picked up some chips, squirted mustard on them, and stuffed them into his mouth. The hot grease burned his throat. Nick was not allowed to enjoy a glass of water as an alleviation. Instead, Penter escorted him out, slammed the back door, and bolted it with vigour. Nick had no time to cast off his apron or hat, so they stayed where they were.

Nick found himself out on the street again with greasy pockets and nowhere to go. How many times had this happened before? Since 'Nick's' resurrection had been rather sudden, he had not fully realized to what extent his appearance had deteriorated. Penter had provided him with a rude awakening.

Going back to the village in Wales whose name most Englishmen could not pronounce did not have its former appeal, so Nick stole into an appliance shop and asked to "see an 'lectric shaver", tucked it into his apron, and ran off. Lurking in the dingy loo of a not-so-popular place on the outskirts of town, known as 'Chippy's One Stop', he found an outlet, shaved, cleaned himself up the best he could, and let himself out through the kitchen, nicking some ham and bread on his way out. Finding a bench under the supposed shelter of a large rock in a nearby park, Nick made the equivalent of five sandwiches and devoured them along with the two burgers he had stolen earlier. A few quick sips from a water fountain and he was back to eating again. His voracity startled an elderly woman who had been knitting a few yards away on another bench. She seemed impervious to the temperature, but gave Nick a curious gaze.

"Wot you starin' at, you ol' flintlock?"

"What insolence! You dirty beggar, and with a Wimpy uniform! You stole that food. And what is that in your apron?" She pointed to the shaver. "Stole that, didn't you? I have a good mind to call the police." She opened her pocketbook, made some notes on a small tablet, produced a Polaroid camera, took Nick's picture with some of the food next to him, and after securing the camera and her knitting, got up and tottered away.

"Go on. Who'll believe ya?" Nick shouted. He mindlessly consumed the rest of the food, not stopping to consider what 'the old flintlock' might do. Meanwhile, the theft of the shaver had been reported. At five that afternoon, the police not only had a complete description of Nick, but also a very clear picture.

By the time Nick had finished eating, he persuaded himself on taking another swipe at the Wimpy Bar. A fantasy began to develop: crashing a car into the glass doors up front, chasing Penter and the stripling out the back door, devouring Wimpy burgers with abandon (with plenty of mustard), and making off with fistfuls of chips and cash. He was to settle for an abbreviated version.

Slipping through the unlocked back door at five, Nick washed his hands in the back sink, and began frying. Wry stares followed his movements, but for some reason the employees accepted him. Perhaps his ability, at least at this point, and his determination to keep quiet enhanced his apocryphal stature. A trip to the storage room brought out the spices again.

Skipness, ever present clipboard in hand, eventually moved to Nick's station. He watched Nick intently for about two minutes, and said, "You must be Harold's replacement."

Nick didn't know who Harold was, so instead of saying words which could later haunt him, smiled, and shrugged his shoulders.

"That be me, Guv."

"It's Mr Skipness. Who might you be? Haven't you worked here before?"

"Right, Guv. Nick. Nick Ring."

"Don't have your application on file. At least, I don't think it is."

"It's round 'ere som'ares. Turned it in."

"Not with me you didn't. Until I find it, do another one. Give it to me when you're done. I'll check with Penter tomorrow. You need a bath." A dull ache began in Nick's stomach. "Well, keep it up, you're doing a good job." Skipness walked off and heard warm comments on how tasty the burgers were. Some people asked for burgers to take away. Another upturn in sales.

Once the dinner crowd had diminished, Nick gobbled down two burgers, squirted mustard in his mouth, and wolfed down chips when no one was looking. He slurped a large Coke to wash it all down. Skipness caught him enjoying the last few bits of the chips.

"No eating on the job, Nick."

"Right, Guv." The last chip was swallowed, and that was the end of Nick's meal.

"It's Mr Skipness."

Nick clocked out at eleven. He felt the chill air and wanted a coat like he had had from the Salvation Army. He wandered aimlessly until he stopped at 'Betty's Bargain Clothing and Sundries'. Going round the back, he opened a dustbin, rummaged through its contents, and pulled out a ragged wool blanket, its colour faded with time and use. Too worn to sell. He wrapped himself with it and rummaged through another dustbin. Old tattered dresses and pants gave way to a large brown coat with a rip along the right seam, about a foot in length. Otherwise, it was wearable. Nick flung off the blanket, put his new coat on, and wrapped himself in the blanket again. Smiling to himself, he wandered until he came to Dobson Street, a dim, gas-lit lane off the main road. Following this straight-as-an-arrow road, he came to an old brick wall marked Lane E. Nick turned to his right and found himself in a gravel-strewn area near a river, consisting of large dustbins and stray cats. He picked a spot between two dustbins (as usual) and hoped their proximity would shield him from the still-cold March air. Drifting off to an uncomfortable sleep, he had fitful dreams of Penter, Armsby, and the Scrap and Skull Railway. For once, the Scottish clans left him alone.

The Catholic church bells woke him early. He dozed on and off until three (the clock tower had told him), when he decided to get up. Peering at a rusting screen door, he found two quid near it. He stuffed the money eagerly into his right coat pocket and began his trek from work in reverse, getting lost a few times along the way. But everyone knew where the railway station was….

A bowl of longstew at Agnes's provided a repast which was modest but tasteful. He left a crumpled bill as payment and trudged off to the Wimpy Bar. Skipness was waiting for him when arrived at five for 'his' shift. He hung his coat and blanket in the back, washed his hands, put on 'his' apron and hat, and started frying burgers.

"Nick. Where's the application?"

"Left it there." Nick pointed to the 'Application Box' in the right corner of the counter.

"I told you to give it to me."

"Then 'ere." Nick walked over to the Application Box, picked up a sheet, and handed it to Skipness. A few employees who had witnessed this little scene began to smile and titter. But Skipness wasn't smiling.

"I spoke with Mr Penter about you. Great cook, clean workstation, and helped to increase sales. But he fired you. Why is that?"

"Naw, Guv, he fired me brother." Skipness narrowed his eyes. "*He* got the beard. Me brother an' me, well, we decided I'd work this job. Hasn't you gotten compliments on me burgers?" Nick had not thought this line of reasoning through. It just came tumbling out.

Skipness could not argue the business points, but inwardly could not accept anything else. He glowered at Nick with even narrower eyes. "Get out now."

Nick grabbed a handful of chips and stuffed them into his already greasy trouser pockets. He grabbed some freshly made burgers as well, thrusting them into his baggy back pockets. Then he picked up a large yellow plastic container and squirted mustard all over the kitchen. Some of it landed on the oven and began to burn and smoke. As Skipness and two striplings advanced towards him, Nick ran over to a large grey machine and pelted them with ice. Throwing his Wimpy hat into the air, he seized his blanket and coat and ran out the back door laughing. A few minutes later he was in the park again, wolfing down the food and smiling all the while. The old flintlock was not seen on her park bench. It took Skipness and the crew a full half hour to clean up the mess Nick had made. Skipness called the police and made a detailed report concerning the entire incident.

Meanwhile, having eaten a bountiful meal, with some to spare and lots of water from the nearby fountain to wash it down, Nick was heading 'home', thinking about the fun he had had. Settling down to a few more tasty treats that were in his pockets, he remembered that the mustard he had used had gone for a lesser cause. But he could not help smiling in some triumph.

The next morning Nick dusted himself off and pondered his situation. A strange, hazy idea began to eddy around Nick's already addled mind. Revenge began to creep in with a new plot. He'd show Skipness who was going to get the last laugh. Hadn't he brought an increase in sales? Didn't he leave a clean area after the work was done? What basis did Penter and Skipness really have in sacking him? This was totally unfair. Marching into the local police station, he asked a detective how to file "a complaint 'gainst unfair labour practices at the Wimpy Bar". It was not long before he was recognized and later arrested, thanks to the reported theft of the shaver, the old flintlock and her vigilance, which is the price of freedom, and Skipness's report, which finally sealed his desperate fate. Nick was given a long sentence, thus putting an end to any hopes of resurrecting another example of something which, at best, should have been left untouched.

# POSTSCRIPT

Several years later

One grey afternoon in the cold of an English winter's day, Ladderman was behind Shed No 6, resetting the stones in the ground which served as a walkway to the side door. They had become sunken over the years, and what with all the other projects that needed to be done, had languished until now. Ladderman had finished all except the one leading to the door, when his large black shovel struck something unlike the usual dirt and debris. He proceeded to dig further, until he had unearthed a singular, very old and bejewelled metal box. Seizing it eagerly, he placed it on the stone behind him and slowly opened the top with the greatest apprehension. Inside the box lay a worn, leathern pouch. He parted the string to find a scrap of yellow parchment, which yielded this inscription:

*"The Skulls are markers*
*Where to find*
*Some buried treasure*
*Left behind."*

"Sounds like one of them old pirate rhymes," mused Ladderman. He was up in an instant, looking back towards the main yard. "Here, lads, come here quick!"

Skulls? What skulls?

# BIBLIOGRAPHY

1. Casserley, H.C. *The Observer's Book of Railway Locomotives of Britain*. London: Frederick Warne & Co. LTD, copyright 1966, page 39, 138, 168.
2. Heath, William. *Major British Poets of the Romantic Period*. New York: The MacMillan Company, 1973, p. 329.
3. *The Poetical Works of Robert Burns*. New York: The New York Publishing Company, 1895, pp. 7, 146, 25.
4. Internet sources:
    a. members.societe-jersiaise.org
    b. www.omniglot.com/writing/jerriais
    c. www.bbc.co.uk/jersey
    d. www.20000-names.com/male_welsh_names
    e. www.amlwchhistory.co.uk

www.ingramcontent.com/pod-product-compliance
Ingram Content Group UK Ltd.
Pitfield, Milton Keynes, MK11 3LW, UK
UKHW040004200726
13854UKWH00001B/25

9 781789 557381